Bubbles at
The Beach House Hotel

by

Judith Keim

BOOKS BY JUDITH KEIM

THE HARTWELL WOMEN SERIES:
The Talking Tree – 1
Sweet Talk – 2
Straight Talk – 3
Baby Talk – 4
The Hartwell Women – Boxed Set

THE BEACH HOUSE HOTEL SERIES:
Breakfast at The Beach House Hotel – 1
Lunch at The Beach House Hotel – 2
Dinner at The Beach House Hotel – 3
Christmas at The Beach House Hotel – 4
Margaritas at The Beach House Hotel – 5
Dessert at The Beach House Hotel – 6
Coffee at The Beach House Hotel – 7
High Tea at The Beach House Hotel – 8
Nightcaps at The Beach House Hotel – 9
Bubbles at The Beach House Hotel – 10
Canapes at The Beach House Hotel – 11 (2025)

THE FAT FRIDAYS GROUP:
Fat Fridays – 1
Sassy Saturdays – 2
Secret Sundays – 3

THE SALTY KEY INN SERIES:
Finding Me – 1
Finding My Way – 2
Finding Love – 3
Finding Family – 4
The Salty Key Inn Series – Boxed Set

SEASHELL COTTAGE BOOKS:
A Christmas Star
Change of Heart
A Summer of Surprises
A Road Trip to Remember
The Beach Babes

THE CHANDLER HILL INN SERIES:
Going Home – 1
Coming Home – 2
Home at Last – 3
The Chandler Hill Inn Series – Boxed Set

THE DESERT SAGE INN SERIES:
The Desert Flowers – Rose – 1
The Desert Flowers – Lily – 2
The Desert Flowers – Willow – 3
The Desert Flowers – Mistletoe & Holly – 4
The Desert Sage Inn Series – Boxed Set

SOUL SISTERS AT CEDAR MOUNTAIN LODGE:
Christmas Sisters – Anthology
Christmas Kisses
Christmas Castles
Christmas Stories – Soul Sisters Anthology
Christmas Joy
The Christmas Joy Boxed Set

THE SANDERLING COVE INN SERIES:
Waves of Hope – 1
Sandy Wishes – 2
Salty Kisses – 3

THE LILAC LAKE INN SERIES

LILAC LAKE BOOKS

OTHER BOOKS:

For more information: **www.judithkeim.com**

PRAISE FOR JUDITH KEIM'S NOVELS

THE BEACH HOUSE HOTEL SERIES – Books 1 – 10:
"Love the characters in this series. This series was my first introduction to Judith Keim. She is now one of my favorites. Looking forward to reading more of her books."

BREAKFAST AT THE BEACH HOUSE HOTEL – *"An easy, delightful read that offers romance, family relationships, and strong women learning to be stronger. Real life situations filter through the pages. Enjoy!"*

LUNCH AT THE BEACH HOUSE HOTEL – *"This series is such a joy to read. You feel you are actually living with them. Can't wait to read the latest one."*

DINNER AT THE BEACH HOUSE HOTEL – *"A Terrific Read! As usual, Judith Keim did it again. Enjoyed immensely. Continue writing such pleasantly reading books for all of us readers."*

CHRISTMAS AT THE BEACH HOUSE HOTEL – *"Not Just Another Christmas Novel. This is book number four in the series and my introduction to Judith Keim's writing. I wasn't disappointed. The characters are dimensional and engaging. The plot is well crafted and advances at a pleasing pace.*

MARGARITAS AT THE BEACH HOUSE HOTEL – *"Overall, Margaritas at the Beach House Hotel is another wonderful addition to the series. Judith Keim takes the reader on a journey told through the voices of these amazing characters we have all come to love through the years!*

DESSERT AT THE BEACH HOUSE HOTEL – *"It is a heartwarming and beautiful women's fiction as only Judith Keim can do with her wonderful characters, amazing location. and family and friends whose daily lives circle around Ann and Rhonda and The Beach House Hotel.*

COFFEE AT THE BEACH HOUSE HOTEL – *"Great story*

and characters! A hard to put down book. Lots of things happening, including a kidnapping of a young boy. The beach house hotel is a wonderful hotel run by two women who are best friends. Highly recommend this book.

HIGH TEA AT THE BEACH HOUSE HOTEL – "What a lovely story! The Beach House Hotel series is always a great read. Each book in the series brings a new aspect to the saga of Ann and Rhonda."

THE HARTWELL WOMEN SERIES – Books 1 – 4:
"This was an EXCELLENT series. When I discovered Judith Keim, I read all of her books back to back. I thoroughly enjoyed the women Keim has written about. They are believable and you want to just jump into their lives and be their friends! I can't wait for any upcoming books!"

"I fell into Judith Keim's Hartwell Women series and have read & enjoyed all of her books in every series. Each centers around a strong & interesting woman character and their family interaction. Good reads that leave you wanting more."

THE FAT FRIDAYS GROUP – Books 1 – 3:
"Excellent story line for each character, and an insightful representation of situations which deal with some of the contemporary issues women are faced with today."

THE SALTY KEY INN SERIES – Books 1 – 4:
FINDING ME – "The characters are endearing with the same struggles we all encounter. The setting makes me feel like I am a guest at The Salty Key Inn...relaxed, happy & light-hearted! The men are yummy and the women strong. You can't get better than that! Happy Reading!"

FINDING MY WAY- "Loved the family dynamics as well as uncertain emotions of dating and falling in love. Appreciated the morals and strength of parenting *throughout. Just couldn't put this book down."*

FINDING LOVE – "Judith Keim always puts substance into her books. This book was no different, I learned about PTSD, accepting oneself, there are always going to be problems but stick it out and make it work.

FINDING FAMILY – "Completing this series is like eating the last chip. Love Judith's writing and her female characters are always smart, strong, vulnerable to life and love experiences."

"This was a refreshing book. Bringing the heart and soul of the family to us."

THE CHANDLER HILL INN SERIES – Books 1 – 3:

GOING HOME – "I was completely immersed in this book, with the beautiful descriptive writing, and the author's way of bringing her characters to life. I felt like I was right inside her story."

COMING HOME – "Coming Home was such a wonderful story. The author has such a gift for getting the reader right to the heart of things."

HOME AT LAST – "In this wonderful conclusion, to a heartfelt and emotional trilogy set in Oregon's stunning wine country, Judith Keim has tied up the Chandler Hill series with the perfect bow."

SEASHELL COTTAGE BOOKS:

A CHRISTMAS STAR – "Love, laughter, sadness, great food, and hope for the future, all in one book. It doesn't get any better than this stunning read."

CHANGE OF HEART – "CHANGE OF HEART is the summer read we've all been waiting for. Judith Keim is a master at creating fascinating characters that are simply irresistible. Her stories leave you with a big smile on your face and a heart bursting with love."

~Kellie Coates Gilbert, author of the popular Sun Valley Series

A SUMMER OF SURPRISES – *"Ms. Keim uses this book as an amazing platform to show that with hard emotional work, belief in yourself, and love, the scars of abuse can be conquered. It in no way preaches, it's a lovely story with a happy ending."*

A ROAD TRIP TO REMEMBER – *"The characters are so real that they jump off the page. Such a fun, HAPPY book at the perfect time. It will lift your spirits and even remind you of your own grandmother. Spirited and hopeful Aggie gets a second chance at love and she takes the steering wheel and drives straight for it."*

THE BEACH BABES – *"Another winner at the pen of Judith Keim. I love the characters and the book just flows. It feels as though you are at the beach with them and are a part of you.*

THE DESERT SAGE INN SERIES – Books 1 – 4:

THE DESERT FLOWERS – ROSE – *"The Desert Flowers - Rose, "In this first of a series, we see each woman come into her own and view new beginnings even as they must take this tearful journey as they slowly lose a dear friend.*

THE DESERT FLOWERS – LILY – *"The second book in the Desert Flowers series is just as wonderful as the first. Judith Keim is a brilliant storyteller. Her characters are truly lovely and people that you want to be friends with as soon as you start reading. Judith Keim is not afraid to weave real-life conflict and loss into her stories.*

THE DESERT FLOWERS – WILLOW – *"The feelings of love, joy, happiness, friendship, family, and the pain of loss are deeply felt by Willow Sanchez and her two cohorts Rose and Lily. The Desert Flowers met because of their deep feelings for Alec Thurston, a man who touched their lives in different ways.*"

MISTLETOE AND HOLLY – "*As always, the author never ceases to amaze me. She's able to take characters and bring them to life in such a way that you think you're actually among family. It's a great holiday read. You won't be disappointed.*"

THE SANDERLING COVE INN SERIES – Books 1 – 3:

WAVES OF HOPE – "*Such a wonderful story about several families in a beautiful location in Florida. A grandmother requests her three granddaughters to help her by running the family's inn for the summer. Other grandmothers in the area played a part in this plan to find happiness for their grandsons and granddaughters.*"

SANDY WISHES – "*Three cousins needing a change and a few of the neighborhood boys from when they were young are back visiting their grandmothers. It is an adventure, a summer of discoveries, and embracing the person they are becoming.*"

SALTY KISSES – "*I love this story, as well as the entire series because it's about family, friendship, and love. The meddling grandmothers have only the best intentions and want to see their grandchildren find love and happiness. What grandparent wouldn't want that?*"

THE LILAC LAKE INN SERIES – Books 1 – 3:

LOVE BY DESIGN – "*Genie Wittner is planning on selling her beloved Lilac Inn B&B, and keeping a cottage for her three granddaughters, Whitney, the movie star, Dani an architect, and Taylor a writer. A little mystery, a possible ghost, and romance all make this a great read and the start of a new series.*"

LOVE BETWEEN THE LINES – "*Taylor is one of 3 sisters who have inherited a cottage in Lilac Lake from their grandmother. She is an accomplished author who is having some issues getting inspired for her next book. Things only get worse when she receives an email from her new editor with a harsh critique of her last book. She's still fuming when Cooper shows up in town, determined to work together on getting the book ready."*

LOVE UNDER THE STARS – *"Love Under the Stars is the third book in The Lilac Lake Inn Series by author Judith Keim. Judith beautifully weaves together the final story in this amazing series about the Gilford sisters and their grandmother, GG."*

THE LILAC LAKE BOOKS

LOVE'S CURE – *Welcome back to Lilac Lake with a new spin-off series from author Judith Keim. For fans of the author, you will be reunited with previous characters, as well as being introduced to new ones. Even though this book can be read as a stand-alone, I highly recommend reading the Lilac Lake Inn series to get introduced to all of these amazing characters.*

Bubbles at The Beach House Hotel

The Beach House Hotel Series – Book 10

Judith Keim

Wild Quail Publishing

Bubbles at The Beach House Hotel is a work of fiction. Names, characters, places, public or private institutions, corporations, towns, and incidents are the product of the author's imagination or are used fictitiously. Any resemblance to actual events, locales, or persons, living or dead, is coincidental.

No part of *Bubbles at The Beach House Hotel* may be reproduced or transmitted in any form or by any electronic or mechanical means, including information storage and retrieval systems, without permission in writing from the author, except by a reviewer who may quote brief passages in a review. This book may not be resold or uploaded for distribution to others. For permissions, contact the author directly via electronic mail:

wildquail.pub@gmail.com
www.judithkeim.com

Published in the United States of America by:

Wild Quail Publishing
PO Box 171332
Boise, ID 83717-1332

ISBN# 978-1-962452-70-0

Dedication

For book club members everywhere!
You keep all of us authors writing. Thank you.

CHAPTER ONE

"ANNIE, TAKE A LOOK AT THIS," SAID RHONDA DELMONTE
Grayson, my best friend and fellow owner of The Beach House
Hotel. She motioned for me to come over to her desk in our
office.

I leaned over her shoulder to read the message we'd
received from our reservations department. When I was
through, I sat down in my desk chair and felt the sting of tears.

Five women, members of a book club in a small town
outside Pittsburgh, had reserved one of our guesthouses on
the property for ten days. Each confessed that they'd all had
to save their money for some time to be able to do it, and all
five asked for champagne to be delivered to the house on a
different evening as a surprise to the others.

"That's so sweet," I said. "We've got to do something
special for them."

"One of the women, Jane Sweeny, said she wants to include
packages of bubbles from our spa with her gift so they can take
bubble baths," said Rhonda. "She said they wanted bubbles,
bubbles, bubbles to celebrate being here. Isn't that adorable?"

"What could we do to help them make their time here more
special? Give them spa packages?" I asked.

Rhonda looked at me and grinned. "Perfect."

My mind spun. "Maybe they'd allow us to interview them
for our special 'Pamper Package Program.'" Even with the
stellar reputation our upscale hotel on the Gulf Coast of
Florida enjoyed, we were always trying to find ways to put

"heads in beds," as they say in the business.

A few days later, on a balmy September morning, Rhonda and I stood at the top of the front stairs of the hotel to greet our book club guests.

Rhonda nudged me when the white stretch limo pulled through the gates. "Guess they decided to go all the way for their ride. I freakin' love it."

I laughed. "I can't remember when we've been so excited about new guests."

As the limo pulled to a stop, Rhonda and I hurried down the steps to greet them. I couldn't wait to meet these women. They sounded like people I'd want as friends.

The back doors of the limo opened, and a group of women laughing and talking began to get out of the car. They looked as different as could be. But one, a woman with dark hair and a streak of gray across the front, seemed to be in charge.

She stepped forward. "Hello, I'm Jane Sweeny. You must be Ann and Rhonda. We've read all about you."

"Welcome to The Beach House Hotel," I said.

Rhonda beamed at them. "We're so happy you're here."

"Hello, I'm Amy Hardeman," said a woman with pink-streaked brown hair emerging from the limo. She turned. "And this is Caro Corbin," she continued, indicating a stunning blonde who gave us a shy smile as she stood before us.

From around the other side of the limo, a woman with dark curly hair approached, gazing around with interest. "I'm Lisa Stein. We're so happy to be here."

"And last but not least," said a woman trailing Lisa, "I'm Heather McPherson." Her blue eyes gleamed with excitement.

One of our valets rolled a luggage cart over to the limo

driver to help with the bags.

"The valet will take your suitcases to your house," I said. "Come into the hotel to check-in, and then Rhonda and I will escort you to your house."

"Okay," said Lisa. "First, I want to get a photo of the entrance to the hotel. It's gorgeous!" She turned to the others. "Just think! We get to live here in the lap of luxury for ten whole days."

Heather, a pleasantly plump woman with blond hair, clapped, and the others joined in, smiling at one another.

"May I take a photo of the two of you right here?" asked Jane.

I hesitated and then said, "Certainly." Normally, I didn't like having photos taken of me, but for this friendly group, I couldn't resist.

Rhonda winked at me, and we stood together for the group.

At the entrance to the hotel lobby, Rhonda and I introduced Bernie, our General Manager, to them.

He bobbed his head. "Welcome to The Beach House Hotel. Let us know if we can do anything for you. We're here to see that your stay with us is everything you want."

The woman with brown hair and pink coloring flowing through it looked at Bernie. "Glad to hear it. We investigated several properties but chose this hotel because of your reputation for excellent service."

Bernie looked surprised at the no-nonsense way the woman spoke but nodded politely. "Compliments like that are always appreciated. We work hard for them. Have a pleasant stay."

He turned and walked away.

"He sounds so European," gushed one of the women.

"I believe with a name like Bernhard Bruner, he's of German descent," said Jane. She turned to Rhonda and me.

"I'm a librarian and love facts of all kinds."

"Jane is the one who got this group together some years ago. She even came up with the name of our book club, The Book Circle," said the blonde. "And that's what we've become—a circle of friends."

"Best friends," said the woman with curly dark hair.

"You're very lucky," I said. "Women being together, listening to one another, supporting one another is a precious gift."

"Women helping women is something we all need," said Rhonda. "Right, Annie?"

"Yes. We could never have created this hotel if we weren't best friends. So, we want you to enjoy being together here. Let's register you, and then we'll go to the house."

Thanks to pre-registration information, we quickly got everyone signed in, and then Rhonda and I walked the group over to the guesthouse they'd rented. They had plenty of room with three bedrooms, a nice-sized kitchen and living space, and a private pool.

As the women entered the house, they first saw the huge bouquet of fresh flowers we'd placed in the living room. Beyond that, the pool and the palm trees outside the pool cage beckoned.

"Wow! This is even more beautiful than I thought it would be," said one of the women.

"We've put bottles of water and a small charcuterie plate in the refrigerator. The dining room is open, and I'm sure you've made reservations for dinner tonight," said Rhonda. She didn't mention the bottle of champagne one of the women had ordered, which was now hiding in the refrigerator.

"Oh, yes. We've read all about Jean-Luc and his delicious meals," said Jane.

A valet was waiting in the kitchen. "I need to know where

to put the luggage. If you'll each show me which room you are in, I'll be happy to carry the bags there."

After some commotion, the valet got all the luggage into the right rooms. Jane took the master bedroom suite while the others were settled in the other two rooms.

"It seems right that Jane was given the master suite because she's the one who organized all of this for us," said the pink-haired woman, returning to the living room.

"Now that you're all getting settled, Rhonda and I will leave you," I said.

"Enjoy your stay," said Rhonda.

As we left the house, Rhonda said, "I'm so glad we're friends."

"The best of friends," I said, laughing when she pulled me into a bosomy hug. I'd grown up with a strict grandmother who didn't believe in displays of affection. It had taken me a while to get used to Rhonda and her openness to others.

"Those women are bound to have a good time," said Rhonda. "They seem very different, but apparently, they've been friends for years."

"Go ahead and make fun of me, but I get a little nervous when things seem too perfect," I said, wishing I didn't sound like my grandmother, who became suspicious of happy times.

"Well, no matter what happens with them, we can handle anything together," said Rhonda.

My spirits lifted. "You're right—the two of us together. Let's hit the beach for a few minutes. We have plenty of time before we're to meet with Lorraine." Lorraine Grace handled weddings for the hotel through her business, Wedding Perfection. She'd become a very valued member of our team.

We walked to the beach's edge, removed our shoes, and

walked onto the warm sand. The salty tang of the air filled my nose, and I inhaled it gratefully as I moved toward the water. I felt part of a different world whenever I stood in the water, feeling the push and pull of the waves at my feet. I looked up as a trio of pelicans flew in formation close to the water's surface, looking for food to fill their pouches.

Close by, seagulls circling in the air caught my attention, and I listened to their high-pitched cries with a sense of rightness. All seemed as it was supposed to be in my world. My worries about the group of women in one of the guesthouses disappeared. After all, what could go wrong? It was a group of long-time friends in one of the most beautiful spots in the country.

I was so lost in my thoughts that when Rhonda elbowed me, I jumped with surprise.

"Here comes Brock Goodwin," she said with annoyance. "I thought he was an early morning walker. There must be some reasons he's so late."

"He's heading right toward us. I wonder what he wants now." Brock Goodwin was the president of the Neighborhood Association and thought he could tell us how to run our hotel. He'd fought us at every step when we'd tried to open it.

"Ah, you're just the two I was looking for," said Brock, coming up to us and giving us a fake smile that made my blood boil.

By the looks of it, Rhonda was as irritated as I was by his condescending tone.

"Hello, Brock," I said.

"I heard you had a whole bunch of women arriving at the hotel and staying in one of the guest houses. I bet you didn't know the neighborhood has regulations about how many people can stay in a rental house."

"I bet you didn't know I don't give a rat's ass about that and what you're trying to do," said Rhonda.

"Your neighborhood rules don't apply to the hotel," I said, trying to calm Rhonda while talking straight to Brock. "I'm sure you're aware of that. If not, read the bylaws of the association again."

Brock made a face and slammed his hands on his hips. "You two think you can do anything you want, but as president of the Neighborhood Association, I'm here to keep watch on you. You are part of the neighborhood whether I like it or not."

"You've made that point too often," I said. "We're not the only ones who think you constantly try to make your position more than it is for your own self-importance."

"Yeah," said Rhonda. "Eff off."

I knew Rhonda was just getting started on telling Brock what else he could do, so I took hold of her arm, and we turned away from Brock.

Brock ran around us and blocked our way. "You may think you have the last word on this and other problems at the hotel, but I promise I'll keep my eye on you."

"Brock, I told you to eff off," said Rhonda. Having grown up in a tough neighborhood, Rhonda was no stranger to speaking her mind or facing an enemy.

Afraid the situation would worsen, I said, "See you later, Brock. And this time, please have the courtesy to step out of our way."

I could see Brock trying to control his emotions as if deciding whether to stay or move. Finally, he stepped back, and Rhonda and I went on our way.

"That bastard is going to make me do it," said Rhonda.

"Do what?" I asked.

"Wring his fuckin' neck," said Rhonda, her dark eyes flashing. "He has no right telling us how many guests can stay in one of our guesthouses."

"Of course not," I said. "He just keeps trying to push his position on us. He's done it from the beginning. If he'd had his way, the hotel would never have opened. And to have it be the success it is irritates him."

"I don't like thinking he has some inside source talking about our guests. Let's tell Bernie what happened. The staff needs to know they can't talk about our guests and who's staying where," said Rhonda.

"I agree," I said, and we headed inside to see Bernie.

Bernie was an impressive hotel manager. His presence and manner were noticeably autocratic, but he was a lovely man determined to do an outstanding job. If you gave him the respect he deserved, he was a loyal friend and an excellent person to run our hotel for us. We adored him and his wife, Annette, who worked in hospitality service for us.

When we knocked on Bernie's door, he called us inside his office.

"We just saw Brock Goodwin on the beach," I began.

"That's enough to ruin anyone's day," said Bernie. "What now?"

"He thinks he can tell us how many people we must limit to either of our guesthouses," said Rhonda.

"We all know he can't. What else did he say?"

"He's going to keep his eye on us, which is nothing new," I said. "But we're unhappy he knew a group of women was staying in one of the houses. Do we need to talk to staff again about not saying anything about the people staying here?"

"It's always wise to remind staff of that, especially when new people come on board. I'll add that to the agenda for the upcoming staff meeting," said Bernie. "It seemed like an enthusiastic group of women. I don't want to do anything to make them think less of the hotel."

"My feelings exactly," I said. "Brock tries to make things

difficult for us. Even after the episode of being under suspicion for providing drugs to one of our guests who died from an overdose."

"We can't let that ... jerk stop us from doing well," said Rhonda, struggling not to swear in front of Bernie.

"On another note," said Bernie. "I heard from Vice-President Amelia Swanson. She has a favor to ask."

"Another one?" groaned Rhonda. "What now?"

"Two of her staffers, trusted men, need a break. They've been traveling out of the country with her and need time to write up a few reports and to relax. I've agreed to put them in the vacant guest house for two weeks, full price."

"When are they arriving?" I asked. "I don't think we want anyone to interfere with the fun the women are planning."

"They're arriving late tonight," Bernie said. "I'll make sure the night staff is aware."

"That'll be great. I'm glad for the income," I said. "This isn't our busiest time."

"Let's hope the weather holds," said Rhonda. "The last hurricane threat died when the system weakened and headed away from the coast."

"We can't let weather forecasts take away the pleasure of Florida at this time of year," said Bernie. "We certainly don't want to ruin any vacations with threats of bad weather. Personally, I like autumn here."

"Me, too," I said. "A few more weeks, and we'll be into Christmas holiday planning."

Having my triplet grandchildren around made each holiday special. They'd be four years old this year and more fun than ever.

"Hold on, let's not get ahead of ourselves," said Rhonda, sounding panicky at the thought of rushing the holidays. "We need to take it day by day. Who knows what can happen here at The Beach House Hotel?"

A shiver traveled down my back. I glanced at Rhonda, knowing she was right. Every day was full of surprises.

CHAPTER TWO

AT HOME THAT NIGHT, I SAT WITH VAUGHN ON THE LANAI, chatting after dinner. He'd been away filming some commercials, and we always made a point of catching up with one another when he came home. Having given up his role on the soap opera *Sins of the Children*, Vaughn was enjoying more time at home with me and Robbie and being close to Liz and Chad and their triplets. His two children visited with their families as often as their busy lives allowed.

Seeing the smile he was giving me now, the one all his fans loved, I sometimes found it hard to believe all the changes that had come into my life.

Life had seemed so bleak after my ex-husband dumped me for the receptionist in our office, leaving me with no job and no home. But good things began to happen after teaming up with Rhonda to change her seaside mansion into The Beach House Hotel.

"It's great to see you excited about new guests again," said Vaughn. "I know how much pressure running the business can be for you and Rhonda."

"True, but it's especially rewarding when we get a group like these women who are so excited to be here to relax and enjoy it. Rhonda and I want to be sure they have an excellent stay."

Vaughn stood up and stretched. "It's getting late. Ready for bed?"

My pulse sped up at the grin he gave me. Even after almost ten years together, I couldn't resist a chance to make love with him. I had known how it would be between us the first time I'd held hands with him standing in the water at the beach.

The next morning, I awoke and stretched, automatically reaching for Vaughn. Finding his spot empty, I realized he must be in the kitchen. Then, I heard him talking to Robbie there. At twelve, Robbie was a great kid into computer activities, the school's swim team, and sailing with Vaughn on Vaughn's boat, *Zephyr*.

It pleased me that Vaughn and he shared a beautiful father-and-son relationship. Robbie had come to us a confused little boy of two after my ex-husband and his wife were killed in an automobile accident.

I got out of bed and dressed quickly. With Vaughn at home to see Robbie off to school, I could fit in an early morning walk on the beach before going to work.

In the kitchen, Robbie was telling Vaughn about his recent computer project. He and Brett, the boy next door, who was his best friend, had developed a new computer game.

Cindy, our black and tan Dachshund, was listening as spellbound as Vaughn.

"Morning, all," I said. I kissed them each, patted Cindy, and announced I'd be back to get ready for work in a while. "Good luck on your English test, Robbie."

He groaned as I took off.

I left the house eager to hit the beach. Spending early morning on the sand, becoming part of the scene there, grounded me. It was there that Rhonda and I often made our best business decisions walking together. But my time alone there was equally as important.

After pulling behind the hotel, I parked and got out, feeling my body relax as I inhaled the salty tang of the air.

A gentle breeze ruffled the fronds of a nearby palm tree, and I sighed. Having grown up in New England, I loved the tropical feel of Sabal, Florida.

I removed my sandals and stepped out onto the sand and down to the water's edge. I watched as sandpipers and sanderlings hurried by in small groups, leaving tiny footprints behind in the wet sand. I was about to step into the frothiness of the water when I heard my name being called and turned to see Jane Sweeney headed my way.

I walked over to greet her. "Beautiful day! You're up and about early. I expected you to be in bed 'til noon."

"Oh, some of us will do that, but not me. I'm used to getting up early. Especially when I need time to think things through."

"I understand. I do my best thinking here. But is there something I can do to help you?" I asked.

"I've been holding something back from my friends, but I don't want to ruin this vacation," said Jane. "Four years ago, I had breast cancer. And just before we came here, I discovered a tiny lump in one breast. I have a doctor's appointment scheduled after we get back."

I hugged her. "That's an awful lot to keep to yourself. Rhonda had a scare a while back. We have a fabulous doctor associated with the Moffit Cancer Center and Research Institute in Tampa. Would it help to see her? Talk to her? Dr. Perkins is a friend of ours, and I'm certain she'd be willing to squeeze you in for an appointment."

Jane clutched my hand. "You're so sweet to think of that. Let me think about it. If I can't stand not knowing, I'll let you know, and we'll sneak in an appointment without letting the others know."

"Okay, that's a deal," I said.

"I've had cysts before, so it could be just that. It's simply the waiting game that is so difficult," said Jane. She looked up as the woman with pink hair walked toward us. "Here's Amy. I'll leave you two and go on my way. I don't want her to see me so emotional."

"I'll cover for you," I said, heading toward Amy.

" 'Morning! It's a beautiful day, perfect for a walk on the beach," I said to her. "What are you doing up so early?"

"Like you said, it's a beautiful day, and I couldn't wait to get outside," Amy said. "I've made an important decision, but I don't want the others to know about it. Not yet. This is our playtime together."

"It's fantastic that you're all so close," I said.

"Yes, we've been through a lot over the years. I feel very lucky to have them as friends." She turned and waved as one of the other women in the group headed our way.

"Hi, Caro," said Amy. She turned to me. "Caro is the only one who doesn't realize how beautiful she is. Her husband left her for someone in his office, and she thinks it was somehow her fault. But in my opinion, he was never good enough for her. She's a lovely lady. Far too nice for him."

Caro approached us. "Gorgeous day! I still can't believe I'm here. The two moms are sleeping in, but I couldn't wait to get out here on the sand."

"Being here at the beach at this time of day is one of my favorite things," I said. "Grab hands and follow me into the water. You'll see exactly what I mean."

Caro took my hand and Amy's, and I led them into the water's frothy edge.

"Okay, close your eyes and simply stand here breathing in the salty air. Let your body relax as you take in the sounds around you. Listen to the birds, and feel the water tug and pull back at your feet in a rhythm as old as time."

Amy let out a long sigh, and Caro did the same beside me.

While they remained quiet, I let my thoughts drift. One of the reasons I was so happy here was because it was how I first connected with Vaughn. I didn't know these women well enough to ask about their personal lives, but I hoped they'd find comfort here too.

"It's so peaceful," murmured Caro. "I'm so excited to be here. I just had a feeling we all should come."

"Yes. I want this time to be peaceful for all of us," said Amy.

"It's time for me to go," I said. "Enjoy yourselves. I hope to see you all later."

I stepped away from them, envious of their long-term friendships, and was again glad for what Rhonda and I shared.

Later, in the office, I filled Rhonda in on my conversations with the women.

"Thanks for telling Jane about Dr. Perkins," said Rhonda. "I know she'll help in any way she can." Though Rhonda had a lot of money from winning the Florida lottery, she'd invested wisely and continued quietly providing funds for charities and good causes.

"The five women seem awesome together, but each has a story. I wonder how it's going to affect their stay. Secrets are bound to come out."

"It could become a problem. I know how difficult it is to keep a secret," said Rhonda.

"We'll see how it all works out," I said. "I thought we should walk down and welcome the two men to the other guesthouse. We must ensure their stay is perfect with them working for Amelia."

"Right. Let's look over the notes Bernie gave us," said Rhonda. "Slade Hopkins and Harry Watson both work for Amelia writing speeches and papers. Amelia says Slade is the optimistic one, and Harry is the realist, which is why they work together so well. They've just returned from a trip overseas and need to work on reports and policy papers for her. She says she wants them to have a good working vacation."

I couldn't help chuckling at the "working vacation" idea. I respected Amelia for so many reasons. One was for the seriousness with which she tackled her job. She should be president, not vice-president of the country. Maybe one day she would be.

"The men sound interesting," I said. "Let's go welcome them."

"Yes. It could be important PR for us," said Rhonda. "Besides, I love a beautiful day like this."

We left the office and walked down the private path to the houses. I sensed a bit of homecoming when I saw the first house, which had once been mine before I sold it to the hotel. It had been a rundown caretaker's cottage when I bought it. But renovation had made it a charming three-bedroom home with a private pool, perfect for occupancy by those who could afford to pay for it.

Rhonda stopped. "You know, this might be an opportunity to improve my matchmaking skills. It certainly worked last time."

"Seriously? You're talking about matchmaking using two men we haven't met yet?" I couldn't help chuckling. Rhonda was convinced that every couple who'd recently become engaged at the hotel was because of her matchmaking ability.

Rhonda nudged me playfully. "Go ahead and laugh. You'll see."

"First, we'd better meet these men. And if you're thinking of involving one of the women staying next door, you must admit you don't know them."

"I'm just sayin'..." said Rhonda, taking my arm and leading me toward the house.

We knocked on the door and waited.

A trim man who looked to be in his forties with a touch of gray at the temples of his dark hair and wearing round, horn-rimmed glasses opened the door.

"Yes?"

"I'm Ann Sanders, and this is my business partner, Rhonda Grayson. We're owners of the hotel and want to welcome you and make sure you're comfortable."

"We understand you came in late last night," said Rhonda, giving him an appraising look.

"Yes. Amelia told us about you. Won't you come in? I'm Harry Watson."

As we entered the house, a man wearing swim trunks approached us. "Hi, I'm Slade Hopkins." He looked a bit older than Harry and carried extra weight around his middle. The man had a swagger to his step that was unexpectedly charming.

I agreed with Amelia that Harry must be the more serious one, while Slade was the optimist.

"We like to welcome our guests to the hotel," Rhonda said.

"And we want to make sure you have everything you need," I said. "As you may know, we ask our guests to respect the privacy of others. The house next door is occupied, as well."

"You can meet them on the beach at this end of the property," said Rhonda, ignoring my frown.

"That might be fun," said Slade. "All work and no play make for boring times."

Henry rolled his eyes and shook his head. "We've been under a lot of pressure lately. But hopefully, this time away will get us ready for the next crisis, whatever that may be."

"How long have you two worked together?" I asked.

"For many years," said Henry.

"Yeah, as Amelia says, you're a great team," Slade said. "Best to have two different views on any subject, even though we agree on many things."

"In any case, we work together to provide Amelia with a clear understanding of what people want and expect in different circumstances," said Henry.

"I see you have a car in the driveway. If you need directions or any help, please contact the concierge desk. In the meantime, if we can do anything, please let us know," I said.

"Thanks for stopping by," said Slade, giving us a little salute.

"Absolutely," Henry said with a bob of his head.

Rhonda and I left and stood a moment outside the house.

"While we're here, let's go see how the women next door are doing. Like you said, Annie, I don't know them at all."

"I know what you're up to," I said to Rhonda, giving her a warning look.

"Oh, what harm can it do, huh? Making people happy is what it's all about."

"All right. Let's do it. I know you won't rest until you size up the situation," I said. Truthfully, I was curious to know more about the women.

CHAPTER THREE

WHEN WE ARRIVED AT THE HOUSE, THE WOMEN WERE on the lanai, soaking up some sunshine. Two were just coming out of the pool; the others stretched out on chaise lounges.

The blonde, drying off with a towel, noticed us and called out, "Hi, come on around. I'll open the door to the pool cage for you."

As we headed across the lawn, we both stopped momentarily before continuing. I knew Rhonda, like me, was remembering the time we almost got killed on the similar lawn next door.

The blonde held the door for us. "Hi, I'm Heather MacPherson, in case you don't remember my name in all the confusion of our arrival." She was wearing a two-piece bathing suit that did nothing to hide a bit of extra flesh. The smile on her face was open, genuine.

"Annie and I wanted to see how you were settling in," said Rhonda. "Is there anything you need?"

"Thanks. We're very comfortable," said the woman with dark, curly hair sitting on a chaise lounge. "So comfortable that I woke up not long ago. With my three kids still at home, I never get to do that."

"It sounds like you're off to a good start," I said, giving her an encouraging smile.

"Yes. I married my high school sweetheart, and we have three kids I adore, but it's wonderful to get away."

"Heather is our other happily married woman," said Jane.

Heather's lips curved. "My first husband ditched me with

two young children, but then my hero arrived on the scene, and we've been happy ever since."

Rhonda asked the others about themselves, and when she spoke to Caro, I leaned closer.

"Yes, I'm single," Caro was telling Rhonda. "My husband left me eight years ago, and I've made a point to be single ever since."

"Her ex was never worthy of our Caro," said Amy, the one who'd told me she'd just made a serious decision the others didn't know about.

We chatted briefly, and then I said, "I must get back to the office. Let us know if you need anything."

"Yes," said Rhonda. "The house next door is occupied. You might run into the two men on the beach, but they understand our privacy rules."

"Have a lovely day, ladies," I said, following Jane through the house to the front door, where we said goodbye.

Alone outside, I turned to Rhonda. "Are you ready to go back to work? We have a meeting with the salesman from our hotel supply company."

"I've done all I can for the moment," said Rhonda, gazing thoughtfully at the guesthouse. "We'll see what happens from here. But Caro is a prime contender for any action between the houses."

"Enough," I said. "Remember, these women are here for a bubbly fun time. Nothing more."

"They're an interesting group. But you're right. We have a lot more to be concerned about than a group of five women." Rhonda sighed. "The next three weekends are booked with weddings, and we have the cancer fundraiser luncheon this week, as well as many other activities."

"Dorothy is helping Lorraine with the luncheon by checking people in," I said. "What would we do without her?"

When we were just starting out, Dorothy Stern, a retired businesswoman, helped us organize social events and get the support of the Neighborhood Association. We felt as if she was part of our hotel family.

A look of glee spread across Rhonda's face. "I have an idea." She held up a hand to stop me from asking about it. "In time, you'll see."

We entered our office and were at work looking over the financials for the upcoming month when I received a phone call from my daughter.

"Hi, Liz. What's up?" I asked, loving the chance to talk to her.

Liz broke into sobs.

I felt the blood drain from my face. "Oh, my God! What's wrong? Is it the T's? You? Chad? What?"

"No, no, hold on. Give me a chance to catch my breath," Liz said. I heard sniffling through the phone, and then she said, "I'm pregnant."

I paused, trying to get around the idea of how she'd handle another baby. I had wanted so many of my own and was able to have only Liz. "That's wonderful news, Liz. I'm excited to be a grandmother again. I know you're worried about handling it all, but I'll help you any way I can."

"It's such a shock," said Liz. "I was hoping to start work at the hotel part-time."

"The hotel will be here whenever you're ready. Right now, you have a more important job. A precious one," I said gently. After seeing how well Liz had handled her commitment to raising the triplets, I knew she wouldn't try to do both jobs simultaneously. Not until the baby was in preschool. Then, she'd only work part-time.

"I know how lucky I am to be pregnant after trying so hard for the T's, but I realize that my dreams of running the hotel with Angie have been given another setback," said Liz.

"It might not be as difficult as you think," I said. "The important thing is to enjoy this baby. You might find a special connection with this child because you'll be able to have time to enjoy him or her alone. The T's will be gone part of the day in preschool."

"Thanks," said Liz. "I needed to hear your response. You're right. I need to get used to the idea."

"How does Chad feel about it?" I asked.

"He's as surprised as I am. But he's not as worried because he's got his business to run. And though he's a terrific help with the kids, the bulk of their care is left to me."

"When is the baby due?" I asked.

"Spring. At least I won't be pregnant during the summer heat," said Liz.

"Does Angie know?" Liz and Angie, Rhonda's daughter, were best friends and a bit competitive. Liz had been thrilled to be able to match Angie's having three kids.

"Angie knows I was worried about it. She's my next call."

"I'm sure she'll be both thrilled for you and understanding," I said. "Let's plan a time for lunch and maybe a little shopping."

"Thanks, Mom. I love you."

"I love you, too," I said and ended the call.

"Liz is pregnant?" Rhonda said, smiling at me from her desk.

"Yes, the baby is due in the spring. She's worried she won't be able to work at the hotel with Angie as soon as she thinks."

"There will be plenty of opportunity for her to continue doing online advertising and other things they can handle from home. Like you, I always wanted more children. It's a lovely surprise to have so many grandchildren between us."

"Yes. I certainly don't want this baby to feel unwanted. I'm ready to spoil another." My heart tugged at the thought.

"Realistically, Annie, we'll have to hang on to our jobs for several years. Are you game?"

Surprised, I said, "Yes, of course. The hotel is our baby, and we won't let it down."

"I feel the same way," said Rhonda. "I'm grateful that Bernie is such an excellent general manager. It allows us time with our families. Maybe we should make him a limited partner in the business."

"That's a great idea," I said. "We've thought of it before. But now, it might be wise to act. He'll be ready to retire before we will, and we need to give him a reason to continue working for us for the foreseeable future."

Rhonda and I stared at one another. "Who woulda thunk we'd be so successful?"

"I hoped we would be," I said honestly. "I wanted to prove to Robert and all the other people I know who ridiculed the idea that we could do it."

"Me, too. Remember that banker who said you wouldn't know how to handle this because of your lack of experience?"

"Experience I had helping to run the company that I created, the business that Robert took over and claimed as his own," I said.

"I'm just glad we went ahead and made it work," said Rhonda. "But, like our daughters, I'm also committed to seeing my children grow up healthy and happy."

I thought once again how lucky I was to have met Rhonda, even if our relationship had started a bit rocky. We were two very different people with similar goals.

CHAPTER FOUR

Rhonda and I met with Lorraine about an upcoming wedding. She also was handling the promo gift bags we'd distribute to each seat at the charity luncheon for cancer research. PR opportunities like this allowed us to do something nice for attendees—women supporting women. In addition to offering free or discounted spa packages, we gave away spa products, free weekend stays at the hotel, free transportation to health services for any woman who needed it, and simple but lovely silver necklaces to those who donated to the cause. Rhonda was also a major donor to the breast cancer clinic.

We studied the sample bag Lorraine had assembled and gave her a thumbs-up sign. In addition to what we offered, small bottles of perfume had been added, donated by a store downtown, along with candy from the specialty shop that supplied us with dinner mints and bedtime chocolates and purse-size leather-bound notebooks from a local gift store.

"I'd like one of these gift bags myself," said Rhonda.

"It's a lovely gesture to the women who've paid for this fundraising luncheon," said Lorraine. "I understand the raffle is for a five-day stay at a hotel anywhere in London, along with two business class tickets."

"Yes, there are other things too, but that's the most exciting offering," I said, wondering when Rhonda and Will would take their short vacation as she wanted.

After making sure the wedding was under control, we left the office, and I asked Rhonda the question that had lingered in my mind. "When are you and Will going to take the vacation that you talked about?"

Rhonda was worried about Will working so hard and had planned a vacation before things at the hotel got out of control, and she'd had to cancel it.

"I was going to discuss it with you. I figure once this luncheon is over and the five book club women have left the hotel, it might be a perfect time to try to work in a few days away."

"That's a good idea. It's something you've mentioned before."

Rhonda made a face. "It's silly for Will to try to compete with Arthur. They own two different businesses with very different clients. Lorraine and I have spoken about it. Since she married Reggie's father, she sees how competitive both men are. And I'm sure Arthur still resents that Reggie chose to work with his father-in-law rather than his own father."

"But that choice has been excellent for Angie, the kids, and you," I said. "Otherwise, Reggie might've been forced to work in New York."

"Will and Reggie have always gotten along and work well together," said Rhonda. "I suspect, though, when Reggie can have complete control over their financial advisory business, he'll be more than ready to take over."

"Chad and Liz trust Will and Reggie completely. They've each told me about the wise advice that both have given them," I said. "It's important for young families to have solid financial advice. The expense of raising children can be overwhelming. Especially when the kids are the same age with the same needs, like the triplets."

"And now Liz and Chad are adding another child," said Rhonda. "I understand why Liz is wondering how she will be able to cope. I'll stop by in the next day or two to see if I can do anything."

"That's so sweet of you," I said. "Liz loves you as much as I love Angie."

"We were so lucky to have met through our daughters," said Rhonda. "What do you say that we take a breather on the beach and discuss various vacation times for me? I need some fresh air and a break."

"Sounds fine to me. Let's go!" Rhonda and I had always found the beach a quiet place to discuss details of the hotel and how best to handle things.

Rhonda looked at her watch. "Brock shouldn't be around."

We stepped onto the sand and gazed at one another. The hotel had become a reality with freewheeling discussions in this very location.

"How long would you be gone on vacation?" I asked Rhonda. "You know the rest of us can handle the hotel for however long you need."

"That's the problem. I have to start slowly to convince Will that he needs this. I'm thinking three days maximum. Then, after Will realizes that the world won't stop turning if he's away from the office, I can work up to longer times."

"That sounds reasonable. The five women in the house will leave in a week or so, the Cancer Fundraising Luncheon will be over, and it should be a slow time for you to be gone before holiday preparations."

"Perfect," said Rhonda. "Before I leave, though, I want to make that offer to Bernie. I want him to feel a bigger part of the hotel."

"I agree," I quickly said, looking up as someone called my name.

"Ann! Rhonda! I need to talk to you," said Jane, walking up to us. "I've decided to do what you suggested, and I think I should see your doctor friend. I hadn't wanted to do anything about seeing a doctor, but I can't sleep without knowing if my cancer has returned."

I reached over and gave her a hug. "I get it. There isn't a woman around who wouldn't understand your anxiety."

"Dr. Perkins owes me a favor or two," Rhonda said. "I'll call her now and see what she can do. She's here in town this week because of our luncheon and the fundraising she hopes to do."

"I must be very discreet about it so I don't worry my friends and ruin their vacation," said Jane. "They stayed right by my side a few years ago when I went through treatment. I don't want to upset them if I don't have to."

Understanding, I glanced at Rhonda, who was talking on her cell several feet from us. If anyone could pull off a quick visit like this, it was Rhonda.

After she ended the call, Rhonda walked toward us, smiling. "Good news. Dr. Perkins is in the office and will see you if you can come with me right now."

"You go, and I'll let your friends know that you're with Rhonda and will see them later," I said.

"Okay, tell them I'm doing research on the hotel for a special project I'm putting together for a group back home," said Jane, giving me a panicky look.

"It'll be all right," I said, squeezing her hand before she left with Rhonda.

I headed up the beach toward the strip of sand in front of the houses. I noticed a group of four standing and talking together. As I got closer, I realized it was the pink-haired woman named Amy and the beauty named Caro talking to Henry and Slade.

I knew Rhonda would be thrilled to know these people were already viable prospects for her matchmaking talent, and I couldn't help grinning as I approached them.

"Nice afternoon," I said.

"Delightful," said Slade, letting a glance slide over Amy, who was smiling at him.

Henry and Caro were standing by quietly, onlookers to the conversation that had been going on between Amy and Slade.

Henry bobbed his head at me in greeting, and Caro said softly, "Hello."

"Where are Heather and Lisa?" I asked.

"They left to go to the nearby outlet mall to buy things for their children," said Amy. "Heather's stepdaughter is having her first baby early next year, and Heather is going to go crazy, I'm sure. I have some time before my son even thinks of marriage. Thank God."

There was an edge to Amy's voice that made me consider her forthcoming unspoken decision. I wondered if it had to do with her family.

"I think it's sweet of Heather and Lisa to use the time to do something for their children," said Caro, and I distinctly heard a note of envy. For a beautiful woman, she seemed to carry a lot of pain. If it was because she lacked her own children, I knew that feeling well. It had taken me years after having Liz to try and fail to have any others.

Henry was studying Caro thoughtfully before focusing on what Slade was saying.

"We've invited the women to our house for dinner," said Slade. "We'll order pizza and salad and keep it simple."

"A sort of get acquainted gathering," said Henry. "In all our travels, we like to get to know people in the area."

Caro let out a soft ripple of laughter. "In this case, we're visitors like you."

Henry grinned at her. "Guess you caught me on that. But we enjoy meeting people. It's part of our jobs."

"Yes," said Slade. "All the travel can get pretty lonely without it."

"What do you do for a living?" Amy asked.

Slade and Henry exchanged looks, and then Slade said, "We're in government."

"Ugh, that sounds pretty boring," said Amy. "What is it that you do?"

"We don't usually talk about our jobs," Henry said reluctantly.

Caro gave him an impish look. "Are you talking about spy work?"

Henry laughed. "Not exactly." He turned to me. "Would you and Rhonda and your husbands like to join us for a casual dinner?"

"Thanks," I said. "Can I let you know later after I have had a chance to see what is going on at home?"

"Certainly," said Henry.

"The more the merrier," said Slade, glancing at Amy, who grinned at the idea.

"I'm here to tell you that Jane is spending some time with Rhonda. She didn't want you to worry."

"Thanks for letting us know," said Caro. "We want this vacation to be about doing whatever suits each of us."

"I understand," I said, knowing the group had at least two secrets. "Thanks for the invitation," I said to Henry and Slade. "I'll let you know as soon as I can. And Rhonda will, too."

I left them as Slade and Amy headed to the water, and Henry and Caro took off on a walk. It was a fascinating group.

Rhonda called me late that afternoon to update me on Jane's appointment. "After taking a 3-D mammogram and an ultrasound of the spot, Dr. Perkins has removed the lump and sent it off for analysis. She said the lump, which was easily taken out, appears to be a cyst but that they need to have a definitive clinical report, which they should have in a couple of days."

"That sounds very hopeful." I had some experience with cysts and their removal, so I wasn't overly concerned about Jane having one removed in the clinic's surgery center. "Please be sure to thank Dr. Perkins for me."

"She's very pleased to do this for us, especially after I told her I'd increase my donation to the fundraiser," said Rhonda.

I laughed. Rhonda was very generous and made it work to her advantage, leaving everyone pleased.

"I have an invitation for you and Will," I said, and I told her about the pizza party.

"Even if Will doesn't want to attend, I'll be there. This is a dream come true for any matchmaker."

Laughing, I said, "You might be on to something. Vaughn and I will be there. Robbie is going to a sleepover at Brett's house."

"After listening to Jane talk about some of the other women in the group, I think both Amy and Caro are due for some happiness," said Rhonda.

"Well, let's help that along," I said. Though Vaughn and Will didn't always understand our motive for playing matchmaker, it was quite simple. We were both happy in our marriages and wanted others to have that same experience. Everyone needs love in their lives.

CHAPTER FIVE

THAT EVENING, VAUGHN AND I ENTERED THE GUESTHOUSE where Henry and Slade were staying, and I couldn't help smiling at the sounds of chatter and laughter. The group was spread out in the living room, talking and sipping an assortment of drinks. Looking them over, I thought they were an attractive group, showing signs of becoming tan and relaxed. Sun, salt air, and sandy beaches tended to do that to people.

Henry got to his feet and came over to us. "Ann, it's great to see you here." He turned to Vaughn. "Hello, Vaughn Sanders. I'm Henry Watson, a fan of yours in your latest movie."

I realized how smooth and knowledgeable Henry was and wondered if he had researched all his guests or just happened to like Vaughn's character portrayal.

Rhonda arrived while we were all introducing ourselves to one another in the living room. Both Henry and Slade greeted her, and then Rhonda hurried into the living room and over to my side. "Did I miss anything?"

"Vaughn and I just arrived, so I have nothing to report. But the group is relaxed, so I think you'll be able to see for yourself how they interact with one another. Will wasn't able to come?"

Rhonda shook her head. "He wasn't feeling well."

'I'm sorry. I hope he feels better soon," I said. Will was easy to talk to and a pleasant participant in any group.

Vaughn and I gave our drink requests to Slade and sat in one of the comfortable chairs placed in a circle with the other furniture in the living room.

Across the room from me, I noticed that Caro had saved the space next to her on the couch where Henry had sat.

Slade handed Vaughn, Rhonda, and me our drinks while Henry entered the room with a veggie platter and a bowl of nuts. He passed them around and placed them on the coffee table before sitting next to Caro. Jane was sitting quietly in an overstuffed chair while Heather and Lisa, the two married women of the five, sat chatting. Amy and Slade were together at the opposite end of the couch from Henry and Caro.

Of everyone in the group, those four were possible matches. I noticed Rhonda paying careful attention to them.

I gave Jane an encouraging smile but could not do or say anything about her medical procedures that day.

"Here's to all of us," said Slade, lifting his beer bottle into the air.

"Hear, hear!" said Heather, and we all joined in, raising our glasses as we spoke.

Loving the congeniality, I turned to Vaughn. "Interesting group, huh?"

He nodded but kept his gaze on Amy, who was now clearing her throat. "I have something to announce. I was going to wait, but I believe it's better to tell you now so you'll understand."

"What is it?" Jane asked, giving Amy a look of concern. "Is it more trouble from Dan?"

"My divorce came through last week. After years of wanting this, and with our son, Nick, out of high school and away at college, it's a huge relief. Our marriage has been over for years. Dan knew that I would move quickly once our son was out of the house."

"What was Dan's reaction?" Heather asked.

"I haven't heard from him. He should have gotten the

papers right away," said Amy. "He won't like it, but I can't continue to support him and his gambling addiction financially."

"Situations like that can be devastating," said Henry. "A friend had a similar circumstance."

"Yeah, I'm sorry you have to go through it," said Slade, taking up the slack in the conversation.

"Because I'm a counselor at one of the local high schools," said Lisa, "I've talked to her son, Nick, about the situation. He was very honest with me."

Amy turned to her. "Thank goodness you got him to talk to me about his father's addictions. It makes the decision of mine stronger." She held up her hands. "Sorry. I didn't mean to bring the tone of this gathering down. I want it to be a reason to celebrate being here together. All of us."

"I'll drink to that," said Slade, and the tension in the room evaporated. He stood. "More wine or beer for everyone?"

"Yes, for us, everyone," said Heather, and we all laughed as the room filled with optimism once more.

As we relaxed, Lisa asked Vaughn about the movie business. I listened with the others as Vaughn answered her questions, becoming impressed with the details of his work filming movies and advertisements.

"How do you feel about fans mooning over Vaughn?" asked Caro.

I was used to the question. "I know the relationship Vaughn and I have and how important it is for us to share quieter times at home. As long as I remember that, any salacious rumors of him with someone else are just that."

"I loved my first wife, who died from cancer, and I love Ann. I have no intention of doing anything to mess that up." Though Vaughn said it to the group, he kept his focus on me.

My heart filled with gratitude for him. My first marriage

was a disaster, but Vaughn had taught me how marriage should be between two people who loved one another.

"Wow," said Caro. "That's true love."

"Have you missed out on that?" Henry asked her.

"I thought I was in love forever, but my ex had a different idea." She glanced at Henry and then quickly turned away.

"Hey, guys! What kind of pizza did you order?" I asked in an attempt to change the atmosphere of this group. One gloomy conversation seemed to lead to another.

"Funny you should ask," said Slade. "I'm somewhat of a pizza connoisseur, and after talking to the concierge desk, I learned the most authentic New York pizza is from a place called Johnny's."

"That's my favorite pizza place, too," said Vaughn.

"What's New York style pizza?" asked Heather.

"The crust of a New York pizza is sturdy but not cracker-like and instead features a tender chew thanks to the addition of oil in the dough," said Slade.

"The crust is thick and crisp only along its edge, yet soft, thin, and pliable enough beneath its toppings to be folded in half to eat," Vaughn added.

"Okay," said Heather. "It's different from what I have at home, but I'm sure my husband, Craig, would love it. We often end up with pizza and salad if I get home from the art studio too late to cook."

"Wait to be surprised. I chose a lot of different combinations, thinking there'd be enough for us all to choose from," said Slade.

"I took care of the beer and wine," said Henry, and laughing with him, I found myself liking him a whole lot. By the looks of it, Caro did, too.

Rhonda quietly nudged me, and I knew she'd notice Caro's reaction, too.

Vaughn sensed something going on between Rhonda and me and turned to me with a questioning look.

"What?" I answered softly.

Vaughn shook his head. "I know what you two are doing," he said quietly.

"We'll see," I said, grateful for the interruption of Henry refilling my glass of wine.

When the pizza arrived, we were more than ready to taste the different choices. In addition to margherita, cheese, pepperoni, and sausage half-and-half pizzas, Slade ordered mushroom and cheese, pineapple and bacon, veggie, and olive and anchovy choices as well.

"There's enough pizza here for the next two weeks," said Jane, clasping her hands together and looking at the selection on the kitchen countertops with anticipation.

"You'll be surprised at how much we all will eat. And any leftovers are great for me for breakfast," said Slade.

"My buddy isn't known as a gourmet," said Henry. "But he's fallen in love with Jean-Luc's cooking."

"Right. He's the best without being overly fussy," Slade agreed. He handed out plates and said, "Okay, everyone, dig in."

I took a slice of margherita pizza and one of pineapple and bacon.

"Sorry," said Rhonda, "but pineapple and bacon is not real pizza. I should know. My mother used to make the best."

I laughed. "To each his own."

"I have something I want to share with everyone," said Lisa. "I'll be right back."

When Lisa returned, she carried the bottle of champagne she'd ordered for delivery that evening. "It's enough for each of us to have just a taste, but it's important that we share this as a symbol of our friendship."

"Great idea," said Jane. "I'll help pour." She got up and walked into the kitchen, but I noticed she was careful not to move her left arm too much.

It didn't take long for Jane and Lisa to carry ten small glasses into the living room filled with the champagne Henry had opened for them.

"Okay, everyone," said Lisa. "I say this is just the beginning of a delightful stay in a hotel that our book club has dreamed of visiting for a long time. It took us a while to get here, but it's been worth every bit of scrimping and saving."

"Here's to Ann and Rhonda for making it so perfect," said Jane.

"And to our hosts for having us here. It's been a fantastic evening," said Amy, and I noticed her speech was slurred a bit. But if what they said about her marriage was true, I didn't blame her for letting loose.

We raised our glasses and took a sip of bubbly wine.

I couldn't help noticing the way Slade was talking to Amy and the quiet way Henry was studying Caro. This group was ripe for Rhonda's magic.

When Vaughn and I said good night, I felt we were well on our way to becoming friends with both Henry and Slade and the group of five women who wanted bubbles, bubbles, bubbles.

That night, as Vaughn and I lay in bed discussing the evening, Vaughn kissed the tip of my nose. "I'm sensing trouble with you and Rhonda playing matchmaker again. Something bad always happens when you do it, dragging you into compromising situations. I want you to be careful, Ann. I love you."

Surprised, I stared into his look of concern. "Okay. I promise."

CHAPTER SIX

THE NEXT MORNING, I TOOK ADVANTAGE OF A BEAUTIFUL day and headed toward the beach before work. Though I didn't want to admit it to Vaughn, his words about something awkward happening worried me. He had an uncanny ability to sense those things.

The moment I stepped onto the sand, I felt better. After partying last night, I needed to stretch my legs, breathe in salty air, and get moving.

I headed up the beach toward the guesthouse area, moving at a brisk pace. The longer I walked, the calmer I felt. The matchmaking that Rhonda and I sometimes enjoyed was a fun way to keep us focused on certain guests we'd grown fond of.

Seeing Brock in the distance jogging toward me, I turned onto the private path leading to the guesthouses.

As I drew closer, I saw plenty of activity at the guesthouse where the women were staying.

" 'Morning. What's going on?" I asked Lisa.

"We're going into Orlando for a visit to Disney World."

"Everyone but Jane," said Heather. "She's going to have a day to herself."

"I see," I said, waiting for any other comments regarding Jane. They didn't know about her minor surgery yesterday.

Amy and Caro walked outside to the van they'd rented.

"We're off for a day of fun," said Amy.

"I told Jane to let you know if she needed anything," said Caro. "We tried to get her to come with us, but she said she wanted a day to relax."

"I'll go in and check on her," I said, standing back as the four women climbed into the van.

After waving them off, I went inside the house to speak to Jane.

She stretched out on a chaise lounge next to the pool. The waterfall was turned on, and the soft sound of water splashing into the pool was soothing.

" 'Morning, Jane," I said quietly so as not to startle her. "I understand you didn't want to go to Disney World with the others. Are you feeling okay?"

Jane opened her eyes and smiled at me. "I'm a little sore from the surgery yesterday, but I haven't told them about it. They know how important time alone is to me, so telling them I wanted this day to myself was easy."

"If you need or want anything, please let me know."

Jane patted the chaise lounge next to her. "Have a seat. There's coffee in the kitchen."

"Thanks, but I'll get coffee at the hotel," I said, sitting beside her.

"I want to thank you and Rhonda for your help in getting an appointment with Dr. Perkins. She has a marvelous background and reputation. And she's so very genuine."

"I have an idea. I know you want time to yourself, but how would you like to attend the Cancer Fundraising Luncheon we're holding today? You'd be our guest."

Jane sat up. "That would be lovely. And maybe I'll be able to contribute to the cause somehow."

"There are going to be raffles for some terrific prizes. Buying tickets would help."

Jane beamed at me. "Great. Thank you so much. And I'll still have time to do my self-healing exercises here in the sun."

"Self-healing exercises?" I asked.

"Yes, something I learned from a woman who did

acupuncture on me once," said Jane. "It involves calm, gratefulness, and determination."

"That sounds fascinating," I said. "Good luck with it. The luncheon opens at 11:30. I'll meet you by the door then."

"Okay. I appreciate it," said Jane, stretching out on her chair as I left the lanai.

As I continued my walk, I thought of Jane's self-healing process and decided it was a helpful way to handle stress. Maybe I'd talk to Liz about it.

I was heading back to the hotel sometime later when I saw Henry standing at the edge of the water, studying the activity of the trio of pelicans gliding just above the water's surface. I stopped and stared at their adeptness as they flew in formation.

Henry noticed me and walked over. "I love this time of day. It's like seeing the world awaken to a new morning."

"Well said. I didn't realize you were so poetic," I said.

Henry gave me a shy smile. "I often must smooth the edges of what Slade writes. It's what makes us such a great team for Amelia."

"Yes, she told us you and Slade work very well together," I said. "Thanks again for including Vaughn and me in your party last night. It was fun."

"It was our pleasure," said Henry. "It's always interesting to meet new people."

"I saw that you and Caro got along," I said, thinking how pleased Rhonda would be with me for mentioning it.

"Yes. She's agreed to go on a date with me tonight. With my traveling and work schedule, I don't do much personal socializing. But she seems the perfect change to my normal routine."

"Yes, she does." I wanted to ask a lot of questions, but Vaughn's warning came to me, and I hesitated.

Henry studied the water and then turned to me. "I don't know why I'm telling you this, but I feel a connection between Caro and me. I intend to find out what it is."

"Sometimes, you just have to go with your heart."

Slade joined us. "Glad to see you up so early."

"I try to walk on the beach every day I can," I said. "Thank you for inviting Vaughn and me to your pizza party. It was a great opportunity to enjoy the group."

"Yeah, it was," agreed Slade. "Amy and the others have gone to Disney World for the day. Thank God, it isn't going to be too hot. That's pure torture in the park."

"See you later," I said, realizing the time. "I need to get on my way. It's going to be busy at the hotel today."

I walked away from the two men, excited to tell Rhonda about my conversation with Henry. He seemed like an exceptional man—someone honest and kind.

Later, I entered the hotel dressed for the luncheon. I loved seeing The Beach House Hotel used for worthy causes, and this occasion was one of my favorites.

I grabbed a cup of coffee and a sweet roll in the kitchen and went to the office. Rhonda was already there, studying the seating chart.

"Morning," she said. "Dorothy called to say that there's an empty seat at our table. Have any suggestions?"

"I do." I then filled Rhonda in on my morning conversations with everyone and sat back as she nodded her approval.

"It makes me glad when we can help our guests find love. Love is what it's all about. Right?"

"Right," I said. "But Vaughn is worried about us interfering with others. He says bad things seem to come from it."

Rhonda shook her head. "Only when Amelia Swanson is involved."

I raised my eyebrows and gave her a steady look. "Slade and Henry are associated with her."

"Okay, but she doesn't know about the five women staying in the other house. That should be some protection, right?"

"I hope so," I said. I hated to be such a worrier, but I didn't like how I felt.

"Jane is excited to be attending the luncheon. She's promised to buy a lot of raffle tickets as a thanks to you, Rhonda, for all the help you gave her."

"That's what women do, help one another," said Rhonda. "She'll love being there."

We stayed busy with several small projects, and then we headed to the dining room for the event.

Jane was already there, in a lovely pink-linen dress, waiting for us.

"I'm glad you're right on time because I want you to meet Dorothy Stern, who has placed several of her friends at a table. We'll be seated with her, and you'll have the chance to meet them."

"How are you feeling?" Rhonda asked her.

"Fine," Jane said. "Whatever will be, will be."

"Jane has a self-healing program she follows," I told Rhonda. "I'm thinking of adding something like that to our mother's retreat program."

"Interesting," said Rhonda before heading into the growing crowd to speak to several of her friends. While I'd met lots of people and made a couple of close friends, it didn't compare to Rhonda, who seemed to know almost everyone in town. Those friendships had helped get our hotel underway.

Dorothy approached, and I introduced Jane to her. "She's staying at the hotel and is excited to be here," I explained.

"How nice to meet you," said Dorothy, taking Jane's arm. "Now, come meet some friends of mine."

After they left, I checked the layout of the dining room, which had been closed to our hotel guests for a few hours to accommodate the luncheon. It would open again for the dinner crowd.

Round tables of eight covered with pink-linen tablecloths filled the space in front of a small stage where the female emcee would speak. The woman, Penelope Pierce, was a wealthy breast cancer survivor and was a generous donor at affairs like this one. Each year, she donated a four-day cruise aboard her yacht to one lucky couple.

Lorraine walked into the room carrying a basket of flowers and placed them on the lectern. I walked over to her, and we studied the room filling with guests.

"Thank you," I said. "You've done a great job of seeing this room come alive for this event."

"This is a worthwhile cause, and I'm pleased to help," said Lorraine. "Here comes Penelope now."

Penelope waved and came closer. "Everything looks so lovely. This is one of my favorite places."

Rhonda walked over and gave Penelope a brief hug. "Let's raise a lot of money. I'm counting on you, Pen."

Penelope grinned. "You're my biggest donor. Let's see who we can get to join you. I see some women who can be a big help to us."

I left them to stand by the door to greet arrivals.

After people were in their assigned seats, servers poured a light rosé wine for those who wanted it, and the luncheon began with a lot of chatter.

I was pleased to see Jane talking to the woman next to her at our table. She seemed to be having a good time and was enjoying the warm bread and roll selections with her wine.

The main course arrived. Arugula with fresh strawberries, grilled chicken, and goat cheese was served with a sweet wine dressing. I took a bite and sighed. It was one of my favorite light dishes.

Keeping to a simple menu, the meal ended with orange sorbet served with chocolate truffles.

We'd tried various menus for the group, but light food with a bit of decadence for dessert was what everyone wanted.

As dishes were cleared away, the women got up to use the facilities and to move around before the drawings began. Servers went through the room offering last-minute chances for raffle tickets to those who wanted to add to their online bids.

I noticed Jane buying some tickets, and then she left the room.

I was talking to Dr. Perkins when Jane returned to the table looking ill. Her face pale, she took her seat and clasped her hands to her cheeks.

"Jane, what's wrong?" I asked.

"I think I saw someone I know," said Jane. "I can't be sure. But it was enough to frighten me."

"Do you need to leave? Is there something I can do for you?" I asked, reaching across the table to grip her hand.

She shook her head. "It could be just my imagination. I shouldn't have had so much wine after taking a pain pill."

"Okay, let me know if you want to leave. I'll help you out of here," I said. Whether it was true or just an illusion, Jane was still upset. "How about a cup of coffee?"

"Yes, that might be helpful," said Jane. "I'm so sorry. I

don't mean to bother you."

I got up and went around the table to give Jane a hug. "I'm here for whatever you might need. Just let Rhonda or me know, and we'll help you."

"Thanks," she said. "It was probably nothing. Just a mistaken identity."

I took my seat and kept an eye on Jane.

As the drawings began, I noticed how relaxed she was and decided the situation was probably as she'd said—too much wine while taking medication.

The drawings were a load of fun as people won things big or small, and we all clapped for the winners and the amount of money raised each time. One of Dorothy's friends won the 4-day cruise on Penelope's yacht, and I hoped Dorothy would be invited to go along with her.

"Now, here is a delicious prize," said Penelope. "A dinner for four at Andre's restaurant has raised over five thousand dollars. Let's see who the lucky winner is." She lifted a ticket out of the glass bowl and held it up."6781829," Penelope announced. "Again, the number is 6781829."

"That's me," cried Jane, waving the ticket in the air.

A server came over to Jane and handed her an envelope. "Congratulations."

Jane clasped the envelope to her chest. "I never win anything. Wait until I tell my friends."

"It's one of my favorite places to eat," I said. "You'll love it."

"This has been such a surprising afternoon," said Jane. "I'm so glad you and Rhonda invited me."

Later, when I won a weekend stay at the Palm Island Club, I knew exactly who to give it to. Liz and Chad needed a break and a chance to get used to the idea of adding another baby to their family.

At the end of the winnings, Penelope announced in a

quivery voice, "Ladies, we've made over $90,000 for this very worthy cause. My beloved daughter, who died from breast cancer, would be so proud of us. Thank you to every one of you."

Dr. Perkins came up to the dais and spoke into the microphone. "With your generosity, we continue to offer the latest in breast cancer detection, surgery, and care in southwest Florida. Speaking as a woman, I'm pleased we can now add equipment to the surgery center here in Sabal. With our affiliation with the H. Lee Moffitt Cancer Center and Research Institute in Tampa, we can proudly say we're among the best in the south. Thank you."

Rhonda then spoke. "Thank you from Ann and me for attending this annual luncheon. We love the idea of women supporting women."

As everyone stood to leave, I looked around the room, pleased that we'd done so well.

"I'm going to take my prize and go back to the house for a rest," said Jane.

"Are you okay after your earlier scare?" I asked her.

She gave me a sheepish look. "It must've been just my vivid imagination."

"I'm glad. Have a nice break," I told her, relieved the incident was over. I hadn't had a chance to tell Rhonda about it, but now I wouldn't worry her.

CHAPTER SEVEN

WHEN I GOT HOME, VAUGHN WAS TALKING ON THE PHONE. He gave me a sign of hello, and I went to change. I had just slipped on a pair of shorts and a T-shirt when Vaughn entered the room.

"I'm leaving the day after tomorrow to go to Canada for filming the sequel to *Love in the Air*."

"They finally reached an agreement?"

"Yes, Lauren Hyde and I will be paid the same amount to do the follow-up film, *Love by Design*. Everyone is amenable to the arrangements."

"You've been busy studying your lines, so I imagine how relieved you'll be to get started finally," I said, though I hated the thought of him leaving. But I'd known from the beginning of our relationship that acting was his job.

"Yes, the director is a stickler for using time wisely, so it'll be great to get this done before the holidays," Vaughn said. "How'd your luncheon go?"

"Great. We made over $90,000 for the research center. I won a weekend at the Palm Island Club, and I've decided Liz and Chad need that more than we do. I'll babysit the T's. It'll give me a chance for some time with them."

"That would be a nice surprise to them," said Vaughn. "I stopped by to see Liz and the triplets. She was a little stressed but was as sweet as ever with the kids. She's such a capable mother that I have no doubt she'll do an excellent job with the new little one. She might even enjoy having just one child occasionally to fuss over."

"That's what I tried to tell her," I said, falling into Vaughn's open arms. I nestled against him, hearing his strong heartbeat and enjoying the sense of comfort he always gave me. I'd miss him so much.

"Robbie won't be home from swim practice for a couple of hours. How about a little afternoon delight?" said Vaughn, tightening his grip around me and allowing me to sense how ready he was.

"I skipped dessert. Now might be a good time to make up for it," I said, smiling at him.

He chuckled at my teasing, and we left the room together.

Later, after taking a quick shower, I dressed again in shorts and a T-shirt, ready to enjoy this pleasant evening. Having lived in Boston for most of my life, I still delighted in being dressed like this to relax.

"Do you want a glass of wine while I get some chicken breasts marinating so I can grill them?" asked Vaughn.

"That would be delightful," I said, scooping up Cindy and carrying her to the couch on the lanai for special "puppy love" time.

We settled on the couch, and I stroked her, thinking of what a superb addition she was to the family. Cindy, the glutton she was, kept nudging my hand every time I stopped.

Vaughn handed me a glass of red wine. "A new pinot noir to try. Full-bodied but not heavy."

"Thanks." I took a sip of wine and leaned back against the couch's cushions, thinking of all that had happened that day. The group of five women in the guesthouse was more complicated than I'd first thought.

Vaughn picked up Robbie from his swim practice, and after he came home, Robbie spent some time with Cindy on the floor. He and the dog had a strong bond. It was interesting to see how much they relied upon each other for relaxation.

"Dad's going away again," I said.

"I know. He told me. He promised that if filming went on over school break, I could come to Canada to be with him."

"That's a pleasant thought," I said, feeling a momentary resentment that I wouldn't be able to leave the hotel during those busy days. But then, Rhonda and I quickly understood how important it was for us to be at the hotel.

The next morning, I took advantage of Vaughn being home to visit the beach early in the morning.

When I walked onto the sand, I went over to the water's edge and was surprised to see how high the waves were. I hadn't turned on the news, so I hadn't heard anything about storms, but I thought I'd better search the news when I went into the office.

For now, I stood in the foamy edges and lifted my face to the sky. Sun warmed my skin, and I remembered that the weather at this time of year was like a trickster at Halloween—harmless after making many threats.

I heard someone call my name and turned to see Amy walking toward me. "Hey, there, early bird," I said gaily.

"Hi. It's such a great day," Amy said.

Studying her, I had the impression that something had changed with her. She moved like someone with a sense of freedom.

"Did you have fun at Disney World?" I asked.

"Oh, yes," said Amy. "We all had a blast. Then Caro went out to dinner with Henry, and I fixed dinner for Slade."

"What about the other women?" I asked.

"Heather and Lisa were content to stay at the house and fix

their own dinners. Jane said she was too full of lunch to have more than a snack." Amy stared at the water and turned back to me. "Jane and I sparred a bit. She thinks it's terrible that I'm spending time with Slade so soon after my divorce, even though she's never liked Dan. She keeps telling me to slow down."

"Oh," I said, not knowing what else to say.

Amy sighed. "The thing is, I love Jane, but she's so unrealistic about love. Her husband died soon after they were married, so she has this fantasized version of what their marriage would've been like. She's never even dated because she says she'll never meet a man as wonderful as her husband."

"And the others?" I couldn't help asking.

"Lisa's happily married to her high school sweetheart, and Heather's second marriage is to a man who's perfect for her. Caro and Henry seem really attracted. Heaven knows Caro needs a sweet guy like him. Her ex is a gigantic ass who's now married to a woman who is all about his money and showing off. He ruined Caro's self-esteem. I don't know all the details, but he did many different things to make her feel bad about herself."

"Emotionally abusive then," I said.

"Exactly." Amy kicked at the sand with a bare foot. "I announced my divorce being final the other night because I wanted to be up front with everyone, including Slade. We really enjoy one another. The last several years have been a nightmare."

"Addiction of any kind is difficult. I can't imagine living with someone who gambles money away," I said.

"The first time Dan went back on his word, I began stashing money aside for a time like this. Fortunately, the house is in my name because we purchased it with money from an inheritance of mine. I've continued paying the mortgage on it and paying for most everything else. Not only is Dan a gambling addict, but he has been unable to keep a job these last few years. It reached the point that after trying to help him, I was no longer willing or able to do so."

"You've stuck with it for longer than most," I said.

"I've done what I could," Amy said. "Now, it's time to recover." She turned as Slade came up to us.

" 'Morning, ladies," said Slade, smiling. His gaze lingered on Amy, and I felt the connection between them. Rhonda would be thrilled by the idea of the two of them together.

"Ready for that walk we talked about?" Slade asked Amy as he placed an arm around her.

"Yes," said Amy. "It's a beautiful day."

"Let's enjoy it. There's talk about a hurricane coming off the coast of Africa and heading toward Cuba," he said. "But don't worry. These things often turn out to be nothing but bluster." I watched them leave, then took a few moments to myself to wade in the water and regain a sense of peace.

Later that morning, I filled in Rhonda on all the news.

"We have two chances for matchmaking," she said with a grin and then grew serious. "With Amy finally free from carrying the dead weight of her husband while trying to help him, I say she deserves a break."

"Both Amy and Slade seem to be enjoying one another, but I'm not sure about it being permanent. If I were to bet on anyone becoming serious, it would have to be Caro and Henry. There was something so sincere about Henry confiding he wanted to know more about Caro."

"She's quiet," said Rhonda. "We might have to work on that."

I laughed. "Stop! We have to let nature take its course, or it'll all be ruined."

Rhonda winked at me. "You'll see. I have a plan."

Later, when I heard Rhonda had invited Henry and Caro to dinner at the hotel, I wasn't surprised.

"Jane is taking the other women to dinner at André's. It works out perfectly," Rhonda explained. "Everyone seemed satisfied with the plan."

"Where are you going to seat them?" I asked.

"In my favorite corner of the dining room where they can have all the privacy they want," said Rhonda with a self-satisfied smile.

I couldn't help chuckling, and she joined in. "I love having fun with our guests."

"Well, we'd better start thinking of how we'll have fun with them if Hurricane Marlene keeps heading our way. I'm starting to get worried."

Rhonda shook her head. "You know how those weather reports go. It's all a bunch of excitement until it fades away with a false alarm."

"True, but as always, we must prepare for the worst and hope for the best," I said. It was a nuisance, but when the time came, we all had to pitch in to protect the hotel and our own properties."

"What else is going on? Are you going to handle the governor's group dinner tonight?" asked Rhonda.

"Yes, I promised Annette I'd take care of it. It's her night off." I sighed. "Vaughn was planning to leave tomorrow, but he's leaving this afternoon instead. So, Robbie and I will be alone once more."

"How's my favorite godson doing?" Rhonda asked. "I want to make it to one of his swimming meets."

"Robbie is doing fine. He's such a thoughtful kid. He told

me he wants to be a doctor when he grows up and that he wants to help old people like Stephanie and Randolph Willis."

"That's so sweet. Stephanie wouldn't like the old part, but she'd be touched by the thought. From hotel guests to family. That's the best part," said Rhonda.

A couple of years ago, Stephanie and Randolph had an issue with their room reservation and ended up spending Christmas at my house with Vaughn and Robbie. Instead of being an inconvenience, it had cemented a beautiful relationship between Robbie and them. With all of us, really.

We went over the budget for our annual Thanksgiving celebration at the hotel and then prepared to meet with Bernie and Jean-Luc. It was easy to attract people to our fantastic Thanksgiving buffet, but we wanted to get guestrooms filled for the event. By offering a variety of packages, we were able to do a satisfactory job of it.

As soon as the meeting with Bernie and Jean-Luc was over, I headed home to spend some time with Vaughn before he left for Canada. It was always difficult to say goodbye, but I did my best not to show it because I didn't want him to feel guilty about leaving us.

Cindy didn't rush to greet me when I walked into the house. I stepped onto the lanai, and as I'd suspected, she was sprawled on Vaughn's lap, staying close until he left. She'd miss him as much as Robbie and I did.

Vaughn patted the empty seat on the couch next to him, and I sat down and leaned against him as his arm came around me.

"I should be home for Thanksgiving," he said. "I saw that Hurricane Marlene might be heading to New Orleans. They're already warning people to get ready for it."

"Rhonda and I already talked about it. When we know for sure if and where it will land, we'll take care of the hotel. I'll clear the pool area here at the house and use the electric hurricane shutters if necessary."

"Thanks. It's great that we have those shutters," said Vaughn. "Using them saves a ton of work."

"I hope it doesn't come to that. Our special group of women in the guesthouse didn't bargain for a hurricane."

"Just so everyone is safe," said Vaughn.

"Amen," I said. "It can be such a stressful time."

"I hope you understand that I'm not in charge of the shooting schedule for the film," said Vaughn. "I won't be able to help except to give you encouragement."

"Of course. You have your job to do. Robbie and I will miss you, but we'll be all right. Cindy, too."

Cindy's ears perked up, and she wagged her tail as if to say that we'd be okay without him. However, the dog and I knew the days ahead wouldn't be the same as we faced new challenges.

CHAPTER EIGHT

As I DRESSED FOR DINNER, I COULD HEAR ROBBIE AND Liana Sousa talk in the kitchen. Liana was a young woman we were helping through college who, in return, worked for us part-time. More like family, she and Robbie got along, which made it satisfying when I needed to work at odd times or when Vaughn and I needed to get away for some time alone.

I slid on a black linen sheath dress, which was one of three of my evening "work" dresses. Even though the dinners were private, with extra attention paid to service, I liked to stay in the background, ready to help while VIP guests talked about confidential matters. It made them comfortable.

I slid diamond earrings into my earlobes, and that, along with a simple diamond drop necklace, completed the outfit. I gave a last look at my image and went into the kitchen to say goodbye to Robbie and Liana.

"Liana said she'd help me with my Spanish homework," said Robbie.

"Excellent, thank you," I said to her. "I shouldn't be too late. I'll leave as soon as I can."

I gave Robbie a quick kiss, patted Cindy on the head, said goodbye to Liana, and headed to the hotel.

As I drove, I recalled our first VIP dinners. They were a huge success for political figures from Washington, D.C., who wanted to work out their differences regarding legislation and other matters in secret. From there, CEOs of various businesses booked us for private conversations. Over the years, we'd come up with several ways to keep these meetings and overnight stays private. I loved the idea of being a silent part behind the scenes for these productive meetings.

I parked behind the hotel and walked through the kitchen to my office to check on things. Rhonda had left me a message: *"Don't forget to visit the lovebirds at dinner."*

I vowed to do that later as I headed to the small, private dining room where a bar was being set up. The governor of Florida was the host for this affair, and he'd ordered simple hot hors d'oeuvres and steak dinners. As usual, he wanted the best Scotch and Bourbon available.

There were to be five men for the meal. I made sure the table was properly set and fussed with the fresh flowers, admiring the low arrangement that allowed the men to see each other without obstruction. We'd learned that important requirement after one meeting that didn't go well, and the flowers were blamed for being part of the failure.

Governor Daniel Horne entered the room. "Ann, such a pleasure to see you!" he said before bending over and giving me a kiss on the cheek.

"And you," I said. "Did you bring Carlotta with you?"

He smiled and shook his head. "No, and for an excellent reason. Carolina just found out that she and her husband are pregnant. Carlotta is beside herself with joy in thinking of becoming a grandmother and is on a trip to visit our daughter."

"That's spectacular. Be sure and give her my best. Becoming a grandparent is the gift one is given for surviving the teen years."

Daniel laughed. "I'll be sure to tell her. It looks like everything is set here. You'll be handling the dinner?"

"Yes. Is there anything special you need?" I asked.

"Just the standard privacy. I'm helping someone in the party decide if he wants to run for senator, so it's all very hush-

hush stuff."

"That's understood," I said.

"Now, let's welcome everyone."

Four men walked into the room and headed over to the bar to speak to Daniel.

I welcomed them on behalf of the hotel and then left to bring in the hot mushroom and cheese canapes Daniel had ordered. Two staff members we'd used before for these occasions would serve the dinner.

After seeing that things were in order and the bartender was standing by, I left the room to give the men privacy.

As I was walking through the lobby, I saw a man standing at the reception desk waving his arms.

I approached him and said, "May I help you with something?"

"I want to know if my wife is staying here," said the man, who looked and smelled as if he'd been drinking way too much.

"I'm sorry, but we don't give out any information on our guests."

"I don't have to see her. I just need to know if she's here," the man said.

I studied him. His dark hair was streaked with gray and looked as if it hadn't seen a comb in some time. His blue eyes were glazed, and though his features were attractive, there was a disturbing sloppiness about him, as if he didn't care about his appearance.

"Again, I'm sorry, but that information is confidential," I said. "She's certainly able to give you that information herself."

"The bitch won't take my calls," the man grumbled, looking up when Bernie approached us.

"I've tried to explain that we don't give out information on our guests, even if it's to verify they are or are not staying here," I said, sending Bernie a silent plea for help.

"It's very straightforward," said Bernie. "Let me help you out the door."

The man whirled away from Bernie and headed to the front entrance by himself.

Watching him go, I sighed. I didn't know who he was looking for, and I didn't want to.

I went to the kitchen to see about the timing of the meal. Previously, orders had been taken as to how the individuals wanted their steak cooked. All but one wanted medium rare; the last was to be done medium.

In the small dining room, the two servers had placed Caesar salads before the guests. I signaled Daniel that we'd serve the steaks in five minutes and received a nod of approval from him. Apple pie and ice cream would be served for dessert, a pretty standard thing for one of his simple meals.

I made sure the kitchen knew our timing and then stepped out of the way to wait for the signal that the main course was ready. One did not interfere with Jean-Luc or his kitchen.

The servers came to pick up the meals, and I followed them into the dining room to make sure everyone had what he wanted. At a signal from Daniel, the two servers and I left the room to wait for the dessert course.

I left to go to our main dining room to look in on what Rhonda called "our lovebirds." From a distance, I observed Henry and Caro deep in conversation and decided not to approach their table. I wasn't wrong when I told Rhonda we had to let nature take its course.

When I sensed it was time, I went back to the private dining room to see if the men were ready for coffee and dessert.

I took their orders and asked the servers to clear the places and serve dessert.

I wouldn't be needed until after-dinner drinks were served. Then, I'd stay only long enough to see that the men had everything they needed for their meeting. I often remained in the dining room from beginning to end, but Daniel had held so many private meetings here at the hotel that we'd worked out an easy routine.

Later, I headed home, pleased with how the dinner meeting had gone. I recognized the faces from news reports I'd seen on television and knew it had been important for the group to have this time together.

At home, after Liana left, I checked on Robbie and Cindy, who were asleep on Robbie's bed. Seeing Robbie stretched out across the bed, I realized how fast he was growing. A pang hit me. My boy would be shaving and talking in a low voice before I knew it.

I blew kisses into the room for them both and headed to my room, where I eagerly tossed off my high heels and changed out of my clothes. I'd just climbed into bed when my phone rang. *Vaughn.*

Smiling, I picked up the call. "Hello, how are you? It sure is quiet with you gone."

"Ah, I miss you already," said Vaughn. "But a lot of the same crew is here, which makes it enjoyable. What's new?"

"Not much. I just came from the VIP dinner. Governor Horne said to say hi."

"I've got to get him to come sailing with me," said Vaughn. "He's not running for re-election, and he's going to want to be able to sail the boat he wants to buy."

"He and his family always visit the hotel during the holiday season. I'm sure you'll be able to work something out with him then."

"How are things going with your five ladies?" Vaughn asked.

"Nicely. Both Amy and Caro are dating the men next door, and it seems to be working for all of them."

"You and Rhonda must be ecstatic," said Vaughn.

I laughed. "We'll see how things go, but as Rhonda would say, there's a lot of opportunity for her matchmaking skills."

Talk turned to Robbie, Liz and Chad, and the triplets. I loved how caring Vaughn was about all our children. I loved him for many reasons, but this one was near the top.

"I love you, Ann," said Vaughn. "I'll call when I can. Let me know how things go with the approaching storm."

"I will. Love you too." We ended the call, and I curled up on the bed, feeling very alone. When he was home, Vaughn filled my life.

The next morning, I greeted Liana, kissed Robbie, and left the house for a walk on the beach. This was an important time for me, and even though I had opportunities to visit the beach later in the day, the privacy at this time was precious.

I hoped to see Jane on the beach so I could ask about her health. I understood she didn't want her friends to worry, but they were bound to find out.

I walked onto the beach and searched for anyone I knew. I saw Jane right away talking to Brock Goodwin. My heart dropped. I wondered what he'd say to Jane and hoped she'd heed our warning not to mention anything about her stay with us.

I trotted in their direction and smiled when Jane beckoned to me. She seemed eager to end her conversation with Brock. At the sight of me, Brock dropped his shoulders and looked ready to slink away. I knew then he must have been pumping

Jane for information.

"Morning, Jane," I said. "Hi, Brock."

"I'm glad you're here," said Jane. "Ready to take that walk we promised one another"

"Yes, I'm sorry I'm a little late. Let's go." I took Jane's arm, and we walked away from Brock.

"Thanks. I don't like that man," said Jane, unable to suppress a shudder. "He's not anyone I want to spend time with, and I certainly don't want him to know anything about me and my friends."

"Keep it that way. How are you feeling? Are you still sore?"

"I'm fine. The initial pain is abating. That small incision is nothing compared to the other treatment I've had. Heather noticed I was being careful with my left arm and asked me what was going on. I had to tell everyone that I found a lump and had a biopsy. I told them what Dr. Perkins had said about it being something like a cyst and not cancer. But still, the thought of another bout of it was upsetting to all of us."

"You're so lucky to have such steadfast friends. Is everyone enjoying their stay?"

"Yes, indeed. Amy says she's enjoying the attention Slade is giving her, and Caro has fallen for Henry in a big way. And he seems crazy about her. They remind me of how my husband and I acted after we met. It was like we just knew we were to be together."

"That's so sweet," I said.

"Yes," said Jane. "It was a match made in heaven, though I didn't realize it would be for such a short time. Still, I remain true to the memory."

"Do you think the relationship between Caro and Henry will last beyond this vacation?" I asked. "It's been only a few days since they've met."

"I think it'll last," said Jane, giving me a steady, warm look.

"Lord knows Caro deserves it. Her ex-husband was cruel to her. This is the happiest I've seen her in years. I understand that Henry has been engaged before but never married. This would be a phenomenal beginning for each of them."

"The Beach House Hotel is a romantic location for a wedding," I said, loving the idea of Caro and Henry being married here.

"There you are," said Amy, joining us. "Jane, we're thinking of visiting the Everglades today. Are you game for going on an airboat?"

"Sure," said Jane. "It's something I've always wanted to do."

"You'll like it," I said. "Have an enjoyable day."

"You and Rhonda, please join us late this afternoon," said Amy. "I have a feeling there will be bubbles tonight." She winked at me, and I realized that today must be when she ordered champagne for the group.

"Okay, that sounds like fun," I said. "I'll tell Rhonda."

"Great," Amy said, putting an arm around Jane as they walked away.

As I headed back to the hotel, I stopped and stared at it. It sat like a gorgeous pink flamingo next to the beach. Its tiled roofs and stucco exterior hid the luxury inside. It still amazed me that I was part owner of this beautiful property.

I moved aside as a duo of joggers headed my way, and then I walked to the back lawn surrounding the hotel's pool area. There, I breathed in the salty air and listened to the sounds of guests on their patios or balconies or to those swimming in the pool. Rhonda and I wanted the hotel to seem like a home to our repeat guests, and there was an aura of a warm welcome about the hotel that couldn't be faked.

CHAPTER NINE

INSIDE THE HOTEL, I WENT INTO THE KITCHEN FOR coffee and one of Consuela's sweet rolls. She smiled when she saw me, and I went over to her and gave her a warm embrace, enjoying moments like this. She was the mother I never had, and I loved her deeply.

"It's going to be another busy day," she said.

"As always. Annette's handling a bridal shower and luncheon for the Vincente party. They'll have their wedding dinner here at the hotel but will hold the ceremony at the bride's grandmother's house. Some sort of family promise."

"I like that we have so many weddings here," said Consuela. "It makes me happy to think my granddaughter will be married here someday."

"That will be a special day for all of us." Consuela's granddaughter, Pila, worked for us from time-to-time on special occasions, and she was a smart, sweet young woman. Though she had no special gentleman in her life, we told her that whenever she was ready, we'd be here to help her make her wedding special.

"Consuela handed me a plate with two sweet rolls. "One for you and one for Rhonda. She's been waiting for this batch to come out of the oven."

I lifted the plate and my mug of coffee and blew Consuela a kiss. "See you later. Thanks."

Rhonda was on the phone when I entered our office.

She nodded hello and continued her conversation. I quickly understood she was talking to our lawyer, Mike

Torson, who helped us with the hotel even before we opened. He was older and almost ready to retire, but he still worked for us.

"Okay, thanks, Mike. We'll get right on that," said Rhonda. "Talk to you later."

She ended the call and let out a long sigh. "Remember that wedding guest who got drunk and fell into the pool? He's saying that someone pushed him, and he hurt his back. Now, he's suing the hotel for damages because he had to miss work for a month."

"There is no way the hotel or other guests are to blame. We checked him over carefully, had one of the doctors look at him, and he told us he was fine. He was quite drunk, as I remember it."

"Yes. Bernie had him fill out an accident report and a release form saying no one nor the hotel was to blame."

"Still, we know how these things work. Sometimes it's easier and cheaper to settle out of court," I said, feeling myself grow tense at the thought. It didn't happen often, but when it did, it made my blood boil.

"We'll talk to Bernie about it. He can take it from here and report back to us," Rhonda said. "I also told Mike what we wanted to do for Bernie. He'll work on suggestions for setting it up. What else is going on? Have you spoken to the 'Fabulous Five,' as I think of our book club guests?"

"I have. We both are invited to their house late afternoon today to share their bubbly champagne."

"Why the celebration?"

"Nothing in particular. They're visiting the Everglades today. I think they wanted to do that before any storms headed our way."

"I heard the hurricane has been downgraded and is heading for New Orleans," said Rhonda.

"Yes, but you know anything can happen with that storm between now and when it hits," I said. "I figure we'll need to decide how to handle the situation tomorrow. We can't take any chances on hurting the hotel, even if we end up with only wind and rain."

"I know, but I don't want to rush into anything until we have a better idea of what's happening with it," said Rhonda. "It takes a ton of work to get everything done before a storm hits."

"Okay. Let's give it until tomorrow morning before we act," I said. "We don't want to disrupt our guests any more than we have to."

We headed to Bernie's office to discuss our concerns on both issues.

Bernie looked up from his desk when we knocked and cracked open the door. "Come on in. I suppose you've heard from Mike Torson about the falling into the pool case."

"Yes, that's why we're here," said Rhonda. "We want to keep this as simple and inexpensive as possible."

Bernie indicated the chairs in front of his desk, and Rhonda and I sat.

"We also wanted to discuss timing for any storm activity at the hotel," I said.

"I've alerted the Housekeeping Department to stand by if needed. Right now, we need to stick to our regular storm, not hurricane, protocol. With the hurricane heading to New Orleans and our being on the back side of it, we're talking about wind and rain for us. Even so, I've talked to Lorraine and Annette about the need for extra social activities should we have to deal with a lot of rain for a couple of days."

"Excellent," I said. "We can offer high tea one day."

"Exactly. Lorraine and Annette have a few other ideas. Hopefully, we won't have to use them, but it's better to be prepared." Bernie smiled. "We're trying to keep a step ahead of you two."

Rhonda and I glanced at one another and laughed. Bernie didn't crack too many jokes. It was refreshing to see him in such a jovial mood.

"I understand one of the men in the guesthouse Amelia Swanson has rented is leaving for a couple of days," said Bernie.

"Oh? Which one?" I asked.

"Henry," said Bernie. "He said he had some personal business to take care of, but he expects to return in a day or two."

"He'd better come back," Rhonda said, giving me a worried look.

Bernie frowned at both of us and shook his head. "Another so-called project of yours?"

"Now, Bernie," Rhonda said. "You know we offer our guests a chance for romance. We try to help things along. Henry and Caro are perfect for one another."

Bernie held up his hands. "I manage a hotel, not a dating service."

"We know that," I said in a soothing tone. Bernie took his job seriously, and we never wanted to upset him.

"Anything else?" Bernie asked.

"No, not until tomorrow morning when we need to decide on how we're going to react to the hurricane."

Rhonda and I rose and left the office.

"Maybe tonight we'll find out more about Henry's departure," said Rhonda. "I hope it doesn't mean he's not interested in Caro anymore."

"It's only been a few days. Who could blame him if he's decided to step back?" I asked. "Love can be so complicated."

"I know," said Rhonda. "I love Will. You know I do. But I'm

tired of trying to get him to slow down and enjoy the day, the family, me. Does that sound selfish to you?

"No," I said. "I'm worried about Will, too. I've loved him as a friend since he stepped in to help me when I was trying to buy into this project. But he's working too hard, and all work and no play is bad for him."

"We don't have to worry about money, so it's about his self-worth and how he measures up to Reggie's father. I've tried to make him see that he's a success on his own, that he doesn't need to compare his business to anyone else's."

"Okay, we keep talking about it, but our business keeps getting in the way. Please, set a date for you and Will to go away, and we'll make it work. I love you both too much to let any more time pass."

"You're right. I'm as bad as Will for letting the business interfere with a short vacation. And if this works, I will campaign for a longer, more exotic one." Rhonda beamed at me.

"Maybe after Vaughn is through filming his latest movie, he and I can take a vacation."

Rhonda slung her arm around me. 'We each deserve a break."

We walked back to our office excited for when we could fit in the vacations we all wanted.

That afternoon, we'd just finished reviewing plans for the Halloween dinner/dance we'd scheduled when my cell rang. *Amy.*

"Hi, Ann. I hope you and Rhonda can come over for bubbles. My treat. We're celebrating another beautiful day here in Florida, and it wouldn't feel complete if you two weren't here."

"Thanks. We'd love to come. How was the Everglades trip?"

"Fantastic, but we're glad to be home here at the hotel," said Amy.

I was dying to mention Henry's departure but kept quiet. When the topic came up, I wanted to see how Caro felt about it.

"That was Amy?" Rhonda asked after I ended the call.

She got up. "I'll be right back."

Rhonda returned with a bottle of champagne to match the one delivered to the guesthouse earlier. "We'll need this."

When Heather greeted us at the door, Rhonda handed her the chilled bottle of champagne.

"Thank you," Heather said, holding up the bottle for the other women to see. "Look, everyone, more bubbles!"

"Yay," said Lisa. "We've had a great day. This makes it even more pleasant. Come sit down. We're watching the news, trying to catch up."

Jane walked into the living room. "Hello. This is a nice celebration."

"Where's Caro?" asked Rhonda.

"I'm here," Caro said, entering the room. She didn't look miserable. She seemed upbeat.

I glanced at Rhonda, who didn't hesitate to ask the question circling my mind.

"Why aren't you upset?" Rhonda asked Caro. "We heard Henry left for a couple of days. We thought you'd be miserable."

"He had some personal business to tend to, but he's promised to return," said Caro.

Lisa put an arm around Caro. "He'll be back."

"Time to celebrate," said Amy, holding up a bottle of champagne. "Who wants to do the honors?"

"I will," said Heather. "I know how."

"You've had plenty of practice here," said Jane, and everyone laughed. "Tomorrow, we're going to the spa for bubbles of a different kind."

Heather slid the cork out of the bottle with a soft pop.

"Perfectly done," I said. One of our wine stewards had shown me how to do that. He'd explained that when opening a bottle of champagne, there should be no loud, fizzling pops, just soft, gentle ones.

The seven of us gathered on the lanai, sitting in lounge chairs by the pool.

I studied their sunburned faces and wondered what stories lay behind each one. It was interesting to see that though each woman was different in appearance and behavior, they were bound to one another through friendship with books and each other. Rhonda and I were as different as two people could be until you reached the cores of us where beliefs in such things as kindness, work ethics, and others drew us together.

I listened to Jane tell how the airboat ride had made her feel like flying, even with headphones on to block the sound of the engine behind her. "I've read about them, but being on the boat skimming the water and being part of a whole new water world was totally thrilling," said Jane, her eyes alight.

It pleased me to see her like this. She'd told me she still hadn't heard from Dr. Perkins.

Lisa and Heather talked about the books they'd bought for their husbands.

"Tell me about your husband," I said to Lisa. "I heard he was your high school sweetheart."

"He was," said Lisa, smiling. "He still is, I guess you could say. He works for a small, local IT company. We have three beautiful children, one in junior high and two in senior high school. As I may have mentioned, I'm a high school counselor. Our lives are busy because all three kids play sports. But even though we have little time for each other, my husband and I are happy." She shrugged. "It may seem boring to some people, but we do all right."

Heather poked her. "You told me you're planning to come back here with your husband, that this place is made for romance." She turned to the group. "Right, Caro? And Amy, you can't deny it. You're having a fantastic time with a certain someone named Slade."

Amy laughed. "It's been a lot of fun." She looked down at her cell phone, read a message, and frowned. "Excuse me. It's my son, Nick." She got up and left the lanai.

"Wonder what he wants," said Lisa. "That kid has been put through a lot with his father. I'm relieved that Amy decided to divorce her husband. It'll be better for both Nick and her."

"Amy has been so cheerful lately. It was an excellent decision for all of us to follow through and come here," said Heather. "It's been worth every penny we had to save for it."

"Craig, Heather's new husband, would do anything for her," said Caro. "He's so sweet. He'd made sure she could be here."

"He's a doll," agreed Heather. "I'm so lucky to have found him the second time around. We met at my art show. He's made my life fabulous."

"They're empty nester lovebirds," said Caro, clasping her hands and smiling.

Amy returned to the group and said, "I'm sorry to disrupt this party."

"Anything wrong?" Jane asked.

"Nick's worried about his dad. His father was supposed to meet him several days ago. At first, he let it go, but it's been long enough that he's worried about him."

"I'm sorry," said Jane.

"It would be just like the bastard to be on another gambling bender," said Amy, her voice filled with anger.

"Just forget him, and let's have some fun," said Heather. She got up and filled the tulip glasses again. "This is our time not to worry about things. I'll be right back with more bubbly."

Heather left the lanai to go to the kitchen.

A moment later, we heard her shriek.

When the rest of us got to the living room, she was pointing at the television.

"Oh, my God!" Amy and I said in unison, staring at the photograph of a man on the television screen.

"What's wrong?" Rhonda asked.

Heather held up her hand for silence and turned the volume up on the television.

CHAPTER TEN

WE ALL LEANED FORWARD TO LISTEN TO WHAT THE newscaster had to say.

"If anyone has any information on this John Doe, please call this phone number. He was found on the grounds of Hialeah Park outside the casino with no identification on him," announced the newscaster.

"Quick, write the number down," said Heather as Caro raced into the kitchen for paper and pen.

When the newscaster repeated the number, Caro said, "I got it."

Amy collapsed on the couch. Jane took a seat next to her.

"What's going on?" Rhonda said. She looked from me to Amy and back to me.

"This is a man I saw at the hotel. He said he was looking for his wife. I explained to him that I couldn't give out any information on our guests. Bernie offered to walk him out, but he left on his own."

"And that's who I thought I saw the day of the luncheon," said Jane.

"Dan was here?" Amy said.

"Yes, I had no idea who he was," I said. "Even so, I couldn't let him know you were here. As I told him, we must protect our guests."

Amy covered her face with her hands and took several deep breaths. When she lifted her face, her eyes were filled with tears. "I missed part of the report. Is he dead?"

"I think so," said Heather. "When you're ready, we'll call

the number. Or if you prefer to do it alone, you certainly can."

Amy shook her head. "No, I want you all with me. You've supported me for years, and I need you now." She glanced at Rhonda and me. "You, too."

We formed a circle around Amy as Heather punched in the number on Amy's phone and handed it to her.

I listened with the others as Amy explained to the person at the other end of the call that she knew the person shown on television. After telling her story and answering more questions, she listened and then said. "Okay, I'll be there as soon as possible."

Amy ended the call and faced us. "They don't have any reason to believe it was a homicide. Drugs may have been involved." Her voice caught. "He was dead when someone found him lying on the ground. Someone may have taken his wallet, but there are no signs of struggle."

"I'm so sorry," I said, as Amy's friends, Rhonda, and I hugged her.

"How far away is this place?" Amy said. "I need to go to him. I'll see that he gets a proper burial. I must do that." She got to her feet. "I need to tell Nick."

She left the room.

"How far is Hialeah Park?" Jane asked.

"It's on the east coast, a couple of hours away from here if you take Alligator Alley," said Rhonda.

"I'll go with her," said Lisa.

"Okay," said Heather. "Through counseling, Nick, you've been part of this situation for a while. I think Amy will appreciate having you along."

"I'm so sorry," I said. "I never guessed her husband would come looking for her here."

"You did the right thing, Annie," said Rhonda. "It's our policy to protect our guests. It is a reason many of our guests come to the hotel."

"Of course," said Jane. "No one would suspect that Dan would show up looking for Amy. They may have just gotten divorced, but the marriage has been over for years."

"And remember where he was found. Like Amy mentioned, he was probably on another gambling jaunt," said Caro.

"I think someone should tell Slade," Heather said. "He and Amy have been together a lot, and he might want to know."

"I'll do it," said Jane.

"What can we do?" Rhonda asked.

Jane shook her head. "At the moment, I can't think of anything. Don't worry. We'll keep in touch."

"Just remember, we have a hurricane headed to New Orleans," I said. "Even if the hurricane stays on its course away from us, it means rain and wind for us. We don't want any accidents with guests driving in bad weather."

"You're right," said Jane. "We'll make sure Amy keeps that in mind. Thanks again, Ann. I'll see you in the morning."

I sat a moment thinking of all the women in the guesthouse. What had started as a frivolous and fun vacation was turning into so much more.

Rhonda and I left the guesthouse.

"Would it have helped if Amy's husband knew for certain that she was here?" I asked Rhonda.

"I doubt it," said Rhonda. "Don't blame yourself for any of this. It's a problem that's been going on for years."

"You're right. The man wasn't in great shape when I saw him. He looked like he hadn't cleaned himself up for a few days. I'm sorry Amy has to go through this."

"Gambling addiction is very hard to deal with," said Rhonda. "I know of another man who was addicted to it and killed himself after losing all his money. Amy told us she prepared herself financially to be on her own for some time."

"We'll let things settle down and then reach out to her to see how we can help," I said.

We went to our office, and without any special events going on, I left for home. I was suddenly anxious to see Robbie and enjoy the quiet of my life there. I couldn't get the mental image of Amy's husband out of my mind.

I was preparing a simple meal for Robbie and me when my cell phone rang. *Jane.*

"Hi, Jane, what's up?" I asked.

"I got a call from Dr. Perkin's office. She wants to meet with me first thing tomorrow morning. I'm wondering if you'd go with me to see the doctor."

"Of course," I said. "Why don't I pick you up at the house? It'll most likely be raining."

"Oh, thank you so much. Things are chaotic here. Because of the storm, Slade is going with Amy. They are leaving for Florida's east coast momentarily. They're hoping to get there and back before the worst of the storm hits here."

"That makes sense. What time shall I pick you up?" I asked.

"My appointment is at eight o'clock," said Jane. "I'm thinking positive thoughts, but if I'm wrong, I'll deal with it. Like before." I could hear the fear in her voice.

"I have a positive feeling about it," I said, hoping I was right. This group of women had touched Rhonda and me from the beginning.

When Vaughn and I talked on the phone that night, I told him what was happening.

"That's too bad about Amy's husband. Addiction to gambling is ugly. It can start with something as simple as buying lottery tickets. How's the weather down there? Will it be difficult for Amy and Slade to get there and back again?"

"That's what I'm worried about," I said. "Tomorrow morning, Rhonda, Bernie, and I will decide how far we go in protecting the hotel. At the very least, we'll clear patios, balconies, and the pool deck of furniture. I don't think we'll need to put tape across the windows."

"What about at home?" Vaughn asked. "Will you need to put the hurricane shutters down?"

"No, I don't think so. And you told me your sailboat should be fine. So, I'll just remove furniture from the pool area."

"Okay. I trust your judgment. How's everything else?" Vaughn asked.

"Fine. Thankfully, we have no weddings scheduled. We'll probably offer High Tea for a couple of days to keep guests busy. And I'm sure Lorraine will come up with some other things for guests to do inside. She's so talented. Once the storm is over, Rhonda and Will plan finally to take a short vacation."

"Speaking of that, I'm wondering if you can meet me in New York when I finish here," Vaughn said. "It's time for us to have a short vacation, too."

"That sounds delightful," I said. "Name the time, and I'll try to work something out." The situation with Jane and the need for Amy to take care of her husband's body were reminders to take advantage of every chance I got to spend time with Vaughn and my family.

Vaughn lowered his voice and spoke softly. "I miss you."

At the sexy tone of his voice and words that meant so much, heat flooded through me. "I miss you, too," I managed to say.

"Night, love," Vaughn whispered and ended the call.

I lay in bed, letting sweet memories fill my thoughts.

###

The next morning, I met with Rhonda and Bernie at seven-thirty to discuss preparations for the storm.

"The latest weather news shows the hurricane is on track to the west but weaker," said Bernie. "I think we should distribute flyers to the guest rooms advising them of the likely increase in rain and wind and asking them to place their patio or balcony furniture inside the room."

"Add an invitation to High Tea this afternoon," I said. "Lorraine was going to alert the kitchen of what would be needed, and the dining room manager promised to provide serving staff for it."

"Later, if the storm is bad, let's offer free drinks in the hotel lobby," said Rhonda. "The Lobby Bar can offer discounts."

"I agree," said Bernie. "We can turn this into something amusing for our guests. A few of them have opted to leave early, but we'll provide diversions for those who stay. The housekeeping staff will remain on alert if the weather becomes worse than anticipated. Then, we'll need all hands on deck to make sure everything is secure."

"It sounds like a thoughtful plan," I said, glancing at my watch. "I'm sorry, but I must leave."

"I'll walk out with you," said Rhonda, rising. "Thank you, Bernie."

"Yes, thanks," I said, focusing on Jane and her appointment with Dr. Perkins.

Rhonda and I walked into the lobby and were surprised to find Jane standing there, looking through the sliding glass doors at the gray weather. She sensed us walking toward her and turned around.

"How bad do you think the storm will be?" she asked us.

"Not much worse than this, we hope," I said. "But we have some exciting things planned. You and the other women in your group might enjoy high tea with us."

"That sounds lovely," said Jane.

"Are you ready to go?" I asked Jane.

She nodded. "As ready as I'll ever be."

Rhonda gave her a hug. "No matter what happens, I want you to know I'm with you in thought and deed. I know how scary it can be."

"Thank you," said Jane, dabbing at her eyes with a tissue. "It's such a stressful time."

I took Jane's arm and led her to the hotel's front circle where I'd parked my car. A valet helped us into it, and I took off, feeling as if the world was being put on pause until we had an answer.

The waiting room had another woman there. Jane checked in with the desk and then sat in a chair beside me.

I sensed how nervous she was and patted her on the arm. "You've got this."

"Jane Sweeny?" said a nurse, opening the door into the room.

Jane grabbed my hand. "Will you come with me?"

"Sure," I said, rising to my feet and following Jane and the nurse to Dr. Perkins' office.

"Dr. Perkins will be with you momentarily," said the nurse.

Jane and I took seats and waited for what seemed like an hour, but it was, in truth, less than five minutes.

Dr. Perkins appeared out of breath and sat behind the wooden desk in front of us.

"Sorry to keep you waiting. But I have good news for you, Jane. The fluid from the cyst that we removed was analyzed, and we found the cyst to be complex with some debris in the fluid but nothing to be concerned about regarding cancer. Having cancer in the same area as a cyst is a coincidence. So, even with your history of having cancerous tissue in your breast removed, we don't need to worry about this. However, with that history, you need to have any lump examined promptly."

Jane blew out a long breath and struggled to speak while her eyes filled with tears of relief. "Thank you, Dr. Perkins. You don't know how relieved I am to hear this news."

Dr. Perkins gave her a sweet smile. "I believe I do know, which is why other doctors and I work so hard to try to get control of this disease."

I shook hands with Dr. Perkins. "Thank you for seeing that Jane had such a quick response. This is supposed to be a special vacation for her and her friends."

"You're welcome, Ann. I'm so grateful for all you and Rhonda have done for the clinic." She smiled at Jane again. "You have outstanding friends in Ann and Rhonda."

"I'm very appreciative," Jane said solemnly.

Dr. Perkins rose, and Jane and I followed.

As we left the office, I couldn't help looking at the women waiting for news of their own situations, and I said a quick, quiet prayer that they would all be alright.

I drove Jane to the guesthouse and was surprised to see Henry at the front entrance talking with Caro.

"Henry, how nice to see you," I said, joining them at the front entry.

"Thanks. When I heard there was a storm heading this way, I figured Caro and the other women in her group might need help."

"When did you get in?" I asked him.

"Last night. Just after Slade took off with Amy," he said. "I understand we're to pull in the furniture from the lanai. Either that or throw some of the furniture in the pool to protect it from flying around and possibly breaking windows and doors."

"Yes, that's right. If you need any help, call the front desk and ask them to send someone over." I gave Jane a hug. "Congratulations on your news."

"Good news? That's marvelous!" cried Caro, throwing her arms around Jane. "Later on, we have some bubbles to celebrate. I think this is my day to share."

"Enjoy!" I said, intending to go home to take care of my own place. But first, I'd stop by to see Liz and the kids to make sure they were ready.

As I drove away from the hotel, I received a notice from Robbie's school that they were sending the children home. Quickly changing directions, I headed to the school to pick him up. As usual, a long line of cars waited for the children to be released.

My next-door neighbor, Cindy Brigham, got out of her car and walked over to where I was parked. Cindy's son, Brett, and Robbie were best friends. "Hi, there," said Cindy. "Looks like the storm might be worse than we thought. I'm glad they're sending the kids home. Better to be prepared than racing to get to them later."

"I agree. Vaughn is away, and because I have to be at the hotel, I will take Robbie and Cindy to Liz's house. I like knowing my family is together."

"I understand, but you know Robbie is always welcome at our house. You too, Ann." She looked up as the kids began to emerge from the school. "See you later. It's been too long since we've had lunch together."

"Yes, it has," I said, waving so long. Worrisome times like this reminded me to slow down and enjoy doing things away from the hotel.

"Hi, Mom," said Robbie, sliding into the passenger seat and buckling up. "I got out of history class. I didn't need to do that report."

"You'll need it someday," I said, smiling at Robbie's lack of enthusiasm. Of all his classes, that one was his least favorite.

"Are you coming home?" Robbie asked.

"We're going to put the outdoor furniture away, then I'm going to take you and Cindy to Liz's. I don't know how long I'll be busy at the hotel. Does that sound okay?"

"I guess, as long as I can have my computer with me," said Robbie. He loved his nieces and nephew, but they could wear him out. At almost four, they each were a ball of energy, vying for his attention.

As soon as we entered our house, Cindy ran to greet us. She hated hearing the wind. Robbie knelt to pet her.

"Robbie, I need you to help me," I said, heading outside.

He trotted behind me. We put down the umbrella on the patio table, carried the lounge chairs to the storage area in the garage, and went back for other chairs. As we hurried about, Cindy raced at our heels, sensing our concern. Soon, all the furniture was stored.

We were walking into the house to dry off when my cell rang. *Liz.*

"Mom? Can you come right away? I need you," Liz said in a quivery voice, and I was reminded of the little blond, pigtailed girl she used to be.

"Sure. Are you alright?"

"I don't know. I think I might be losing the baby."

"Robbie, Cindy, and I are on our way," I said, motioning Robbie to come with me. He snapped a leash on Cindy's collar, and they left.

"Have you called Dr. Benson?" I asked Liz. Ruth Benson was the best OBGYN doctor in the entire area. She'd delivered the triplets with a team of doctors and had welcomed all of Rhonda's and Angela's children.

"I'm waiting to hear from her," said Liz. "I'm so scared."

"I'm on my way," I said, locking the door behind me.

CHAPTER ELEVEN

WHEN WE ARRIVED AT LIZ'S HOUSE, THE TRIPLETS WERE in the playroom, busy playing with a tube of toothpaste one of them must have retrieved from the master bathroom. Their toothpaste-streaked faces lit up at the sight of us.

Noah went for the dog, Emma went for Robbie, and Olivia lifted her arms to me.

I picked her up and carried her to Liz's room, where I found her lying on her bed, tears trailing down her cheeks.

She looked up at Olivia. "Oh, my word. What have you three been up to now?"

Olivia patted her cheeks. "Pretty."

"No," I said. "It's for your teeth." I set her down. "Go with the others. I'll be right there."

I sat on the edge of the bed and took hold of Liz's hand. "Tell me what's going on."

"I'm spotting," said Liz. "I've felt so tired lately. I'm worried this baby isn't going to stay with me."

"Try Dr. Benson's office again. Did you tell them what was happening?"

"I just said I needed Dr. Benson's advice," said Liz. "I was crying too hard to say more."

"Oh, here's her office calling you now." I handed the cell phone to Liz.

"Hi, Dr. Benson," said Liz, trying not to cry. "My mom is here, and I'm putting you on speaker phone, okay?"

"Certainly. Now tell me, what's going on?" Dr. Benson answered calmly.

Liz gave the doctor the details. "Is it true hurricanes can cause women to go into labor? Is the storm doing this to me?"

"There has long been anecdotal evidence of early labor and delivery in severe weather events leading to preterm birth. Significant barometric pressure changes are associated with hurricanes. But I don't think that's the case here," said Dr. Benson kindly. "The first trimester can be tricky because of the changes to your body. Nature has a way of determining the viability of any pregnancy. I need to know exactly what's going on with you."

I listened as Liz gave Dr. Benson more details.

"Having three children under the age of four is difficult for anyone. I think the best you can do is take it easy as much as possible. I'm sure your mother will help you. Right, Ann?"

"Oh, yes," I said. "I'll see that she has help."

"Try not to lift the children, and let's see if this bit of rest will make a difference. What you've told me so far doesn't make me believe that you're having a miscarriage. But as soon as any changes take place, you're to come right into the office to see me. You're a strong, healthy woman, Liz. It's common for some light spotting to occur. I'm here if you need me."

The call ended, and I hugged Liz. "Let's take care of you, and we'll let nature do its job."

Tears streamed down Liz's face. "I feel so guilty about not wanting this baby at first. Maybe this is my punishment for feeling that way."

I lifted her chin and made her look at me. "I don't believe life works that way. Do you?"

Liz shook her head. "I guess not." She caressed her stomach. "I promise to love this baby."

"I have no doubt you will. I know you and Chad were surprised about it, but that's all your reaction was. Surprise. Not anything awful. Look at the way you're caressing your stomach. You're already protecting this baby. That's love, honey."

Liz drew a deep breath. "I don't care if it's a boy or a girl. I just want this baby to be part of our family."

"I know you do," I said, hugging her. "Now, let's see how the T's are doing. Thank God, toothpaste is washable."

"What about help for the next few days?" Liz said. "I know you'll be busy at the hotel with the storm."

"Why don't I call Liana and see if she can stay here all week instead of working part-time for each of us? I'm sure I can get help with Robbie if needed."

"Thanks. That would be such a relief. Liana is at class right now but should be here sometime soon." Liz grinned. "In the meantime, my little brother might be very busy."

"I'll explain he needs to help," I said, giving her a last, comforting squeeze. "Now, you rest as much as you can."

I left her and went to the playroom.

"How about a snack?" I asked the triplets, opening the gate to their playroom.

They jumped to their feet and headed for the kitchen. They climbed into their booster seats, and while they were busy eating, I washed each sweet little face.

Robbie sat with the triplets, eager for a snack, too.

I quietly explained to Robbie that Liz would have to rest as much as possible, so it would be up to him to play with the triplets until Liana came to help.

Robbie gave me a solemn look. "Can I go see Lizzie?"

"Of course," I said, pleased they shared a special bond. My ex had fathered them both. And though he'd thought Liz would raise Robbie if anything happened to him and Kandie, she was too young to be able to do so, which is why Vaughn and I had adopted him. It had turned out to be a perfect solution.

When the triplets finished their snack, I rewashed their faces and hands and led them into the playroom, where they could each choose a book for Robbie to read.

Once Robbie was seated with them, I locked the gate to the playroom and said, "I'll be back as soon as I can. Liz is right here. I don't want her lifting the children."

"Okay, I can do this," said Robbie. "Lizzie told me not to worry. We'd all be fine. Uncle Chad is on his way home."

Cindy was curled up between Noah and Olivia, and Emma was sitting next to Robbie, holding a book for him.

At the touching scene, I blinked away sentimental tears and turned to go.

At the hotel, things were chaotic. The lobby was filled with guests milling around. I noticed that a coffee service had been refreshed and now held plates of cookies.

I went to Bernie's office and found Rhonda there, along with various department heads.

"Thanks for joining us, Ann. Everything all right at home?" said Bernie.

"Yes, thank you. What's going on?" I answered.

Bernie briefed me on each hotel department's chores. "In a matter of hours, things have become more serious than we'd thought. Housekeeping will see that all the patios, balconies, and the pool deck are cleared of furniture. The same goes for the sunset deck. The beach chairs have already been stacked and tied together."

"We have the library set for high tea today and tomorrow," said Lorraine. "We've also planned a few party games for those who might be interested, and we're having special cocktail hours both days."

"The kitchen is aware of all these plans," said Bernie,

answering my silent question. "Manny and his crew are doing what they can to prepare the landscaping."

"When are we going to get the worst of it?" I asked.

"It's forecast to hit east of New Orleans in a few hours," said Bernie. "We'll post extra security during the night in case we need help."

"Thank you, everyone, for all your help. It's times like this when it counts to have a cooperative team," I said.

"We appreciate all of you," added Rhonda.

"Okay, then, we will meet back in my office in a few hours for updates," said Bernie.

We all rose.

Rhonda pulled me aside. "Let's talk to the women in the guesthouse. I want to know if Amy made it back from seeing to her ex."

We went to our office and called Jane.

"How are things with Amy? Is she back yet?" Rhonda asked her, putting her on the speaker phone.

"No, she and Slade are staying there. Amy's son, Nick, is flying into Miami from Philadelphia, where he attends the University of Pennsylvania. They're making some family decisions there."

"So, they'll wait until after the storm hits here," I said. "Right?"

"Yes," said Jane. "Slade can stay with her. After the details are taken care of, he'll bring her back here. Amy told us she doesn't know what she'd do without him. He's been so supportive of her."

Rhonda and I glanced at one another.

"No matter what happens, Amy says they'll be friends forever," Jane added.

I couldn't help repeating Rhonda's smile at that bit of news. "I'm sorry about what happened, but maybe some good will come from it. Will Amy's son return with them?"

"No, he'll go right back to school. It's a critical time for him. Besides, Nick has been through a lot with his father for several years. He might need both the time alone and the diversion of school."

"I understand." I was someone who needed to work through my feelings alone, at least initially.

"I'm going to go home and make sure everything is set there," said Rhonda. "Rita's cousin will take care of the landscaping and getting everything cleared off the patio and the balcony." Rita Ramos was Rhonda's housekeeper and had been with her since her marriage to Will. Her sister, Elena, had worked for me before she got married and went into business with her husband, who ran a few spas in the area. They were a terrific family.

I told Rhonda about Liz and said, "I'll check in with her to make sure everything is all right, and then I'll work here until things have settled down a bit. It'll be helpful to see how many people sign up for high tea. I'll work on some ideas for Christmas high tea services. Inviting someone to the hotel for high tea is a delightful holiday gift."

"Maybe we can get a deal on holiday chinaware," said Rhonda. "That will add to its glamour."

"See you later. But if Bernie doesn't think it's necessary for us to stay, I'll call you. We might be needed more tomorrow when there will be cleanup and assessments to do."

"Yes," said Rhonda. "That makes more sense. Good luck with everything."

"You, too," I said.

After working for a few hours and assessing the situation outdoors, I decided I'd feel better about riding out the storm at home with Robbie and Cindy. Liz needed the quiet without having guests in her house.

As I headed out of the office, the palm tree fronds were whipping around in the wind, and the sound of the rain hitting the windows was more like angry slaps.

I drove to Liz's to pick up Robbie and Cindy and to make sure my daughter was okay. Liz wasn't usually emotional, but earlier, I could tell she was at her wit's end with worry.

I parked as close to the front door as I could and dashed through the rain. Robbie answered it and held a finger to his lips. "The T's are finally down for a late nap."

When I walked into the kitchen, I found Chad alone. "Where's Liana?" I asked.

"She went home to help her family get ready for the storm. They grow vegetables for the local markets, and they're trying to do what they can to save them from being ruined by the wind and rain."

"How's Liz?" I asked.

"Asleep," said Chad. "We think she's going to be alright, but she'll never forgive herself if she doesn't do everything the doctor said and then have something go wrong."

"I understand," I said. "How are you feeling about what's happening?"

"I think Liz and the baby are going to be fine. Liz feels bad because we remember how excited we were to think we would have a baby before we found out we were having triplets. It's different this time, but it doesn't mean we don't want this baby."

I gave him a quick hug. "I love that you support Liz like you do. I'm going to leave with Robbie and Cindy to go back home. I think I need to be there in case anything goes wrong."

"Vaughn's boat is going to be okay?"

"He thinks so. We're lucky that we live inside an inlet. It

protects the boat."

I tiptoed to Liz's room and peered inside.

She was lying on the bed curled up like she used to do as a child, holding onto one of Olivia's Teddy bears. Tears stung my eyes. She'd always been resilient, but I knew if this situation went bad, it would break her heart. I blew a kiss into the room and went to get Robbie and Cindy.

CHAPTER TWELVE

AT HOME, THE FLOWERS BORDERING THE SHRUBBERY IN front of the house bowed their heads against the rain and wind, drooping pathetically. A frond from one of the palm trees had dropped to the ground. I figured by the time the storm was over, it wouldn't be the only one lying there.

Robbie, Cindy, and I hurried inside. Instead of being on the lanai as we usually were at this time of day, we stayed in Vaughn's den. The paneled room gave us a feeling of being protected because there was only one window.

While I sat on the couch and read, Cindy snuggled up against me. Robbie remained on the floor, his back against the sofa, playing a computer game.

I sent Vaughn a message to tell him we were there and then called Bernie to make sure things were all right at the hotel.

At his direction, I called Rhonda and told her Bernie didn't need us at the hotel. He would stay on the couch in his office for as long as necessary.

"Fabulous," Rhonda said when I relayed the message. "Drew is not feeling well, and I encouraged Rita to go home to be with her family."

I fixed a simple salad with grilled chicken for dinner, and when it was time, I joined Cindy and Robbie, who had stretched out on my bed to watch a movie with me before they settled in Robbie's room.

During the night, I moved restlessly, matching the mood of the outdoors scene. By morning, things were much quieter, though it continued to rain. Flooding issues concerned us the most now.

I wrapped my robe around me and looked out at the backyard, where Vaughn's boat was tied to our dock. It seemed to be doing okay now that the water had calmed.

A few more palm fronds were lying here and there, but all had borne the storm better than I'd thought.

School was still closed for the day, so after I got ready to go to the hotel, I made sure Robbie had breakfast and was safely next door at his best friend's house before I headed to work.

On the way, I called Liz to see how she was doing.

"I'm feeling much better," said Liz. "Chad is making sure I lay low for the rest of the week by staying home to work. And Liana is coming in this morning."

"I'm so relieved," I said. "You know I'm here to help if you need me. I love you."

"Love you too. Thanks, Mom. It means a lot."

I ended the call and pulled into the hotel, stopping by the front gate to assess the damage.

Surprisingly, there was little. Manny had put up warning signs in a couple of places where rainwater in the grass had pooled. But aside from drooping plants that would, no doubt, return to normal after sunlight helped to restore them, the lawn only needed to be cleared of debris.

I pulled behind the hotel and parked.

When I went into the kitchen, I found Consuela in charge as usual.

" 'Morning," I called to her cheerfully. "Thankfully, we don't have much damage. Manny and his crew did a great job of preparing for the weather." We hugged, and then I grabbed a cup of coffee and went into my office.

Rhonda called me, and we decided she'd stay at home until Drew was feeling better.

"I know whenever I got sick as a child, I always felt better if my mother was around," said Rhonda. "I'll come to the office this afternoon if I can. Otherwise, I'll see you tomorrow. Let me know how our "Fab Five" women are doing."

"Will do," I said.

After taking care of messages, I headed to the guesthouses to see what was going on there, assessing any damage to the property along the way.

I walked along the beach so I could inspect our sunset deck for any damage. What had started as a simple wooden deck had turned into an attractive, covered facility that provided food and drinks all day to our beachgoers, closing after the sun went down. It generated a satisfying income for us and provided a place for our guests to watch the famous Florida west coast sunsets. It also sometimes served as a beach wedding location.

A couple of staffers were sweeping sand off the deck and cleaning up broken branches of nearby shrubbery.

I stopped to say hello and to thank them for their help before going on my way.

During and after a windstorm, the beach filled with treasures tossed upon the sand by the pounding water. The beach was now filled with people stooped over, searching for finds. Even walking past them, I found myself looking down to see if I could spot something special.

The salty smell of the air held a freshness that followed a storm. I stopped and studied the white-capped waves rolling into the shore with a fury they normally lacked. Seagulls and terns screeched their excitement and dove for their own treasures that the ruffled waters offered up.

Before I reached the path to the guesthouses, I saw Jane, Heather, and Lisa looking for shells together.

I approached them. "Find any unusual ones?"

They saw me and grinned.

"I found a scallop and a couple of olive shells," said Jane, holding them up.

"I got a worm shell and a sundial," said Heather.

"We're using a book to identify them," Lisa said, holding up a small paperback.

"Of course you are," I said, smiling. "You're book club members."

Lisa laughed, then grew serious. "How's everything at the hotel? We're going to go to another high tea this afternoon. The one yesterday was fabulous."

"Yes, so much fun," said Heather. "I've got to get a recipe for those little buttercakes."

"You can try," I said. "Ask Annette for it."

"What's the story with Amy? And where is Caro?" I asked.

"Amy and Slade are still in Miami with her son," said Jane. "They're arranging to have Dan's body cremated. Both Amy and Nick wanted to honor Dan's wishes. Amy will retrieve the ashes sometime later."

"That seems like a thought-out plan," I said. "How about Caro? What's happening with her?"

The three women glanced at one another.

Finally, Heather said, "We haven't seen much of her. She and Henry have camped out at his house. I've never seen Caro so happy."

Lisa added, "I think it's the best thing to happen to her in a long time. I hope it continues long after we leave."

"Don't talk about leaving," teased Heather. "I don't want to think about returning to my usual routine after enjoying the luxury here."

"Have you spent time at the spa yet? You've talked about it," I said.

"Yes, but it never happened. We've signed up for a day at the spa tomorrow, so Amy is here to enjoy it with us."

"Be sure to sign up time in the sauna," I said. "Have luck with your treasure hunts."

As I headed back to the hotel, I saw Brock Goodwin in the distance and decided to jog. He was the last person I wanted to meet up with.

As luck would have it, by the time I got to the sunset deck, he was calling to me as he ran in my direction. "Ann! Wait!"

With no other choice but to face him, I stopped and waited for him to approach.

"Hello, Brock," I said. "What are you doing out on the beach? I would think you'd be busy assessing property damage in the neighborhood."

"That's what I want to talk to you about. I'm wondering if you'd be neighborly and offer your landscaping services to the neighborhood. You're doing so well with the hotel that you should be able to afford to pay your staff to work for me for a while."

I held my breath and counted to three, grateful Rhonda wasn't with me. Someday, she'd get her wish and wring Brock's neck because he cared only about himself and his self-created reputation of being someone important.

"You know we can't do that. Besides, I could never make such a commitment without approval from both our hotel manager and the head of our landscaping team."

"Manny Sanchez would never agree to help me," said Brock.

"Oh, that's right," I said, acting innocent. "It has something to do with the names you've called him upon occasion."

"Well, I ..." began Brock.

"Besides, I thought the Neighborhood Association had a contract with a landscaping company," I said. "What happened? They don't want to work for you either?"

"Well, I ..." began Brock again.

I held up my hand to stop him. " 'Nuff said. As you may imagine, I'm busy with the hotel. See you around, Brock. Maybe someone on the board has a better idea. You should try talking to them."

Brock made a face and glared at me before he turned and walked away.

I knew very well that if he went to a board member about his troubles with the landscapers, they might find it an excuse to fire him. If only someone else wanted the job.

I talked with Bernie inside the hotel, who confirmed what I had suspected: things were in order.

At my urging, he finally agreed to go home to rest. Lorraine was in charge of another high tea, and we were continuing with a storm-inspired special cocktail hour in the lobby. Tomorrow, things would be back to normal.

Before I went home that afternoon, I walked over to the guesthouse to talk to Amy. Jane had texted me that she and Slade were back from Miami.

When I arrived, Amy was sitting on the couch surrounded by her friends. She smiled at me when I walked into the living room. "Hi, Ann."

"I'm here to see how you're doing," I said. "How did things go?"

Amy looked forlorn. "It was very sad and emotional for both my son and me. Such a waste of a man who once had so much to offer us and the world. I'm glad we're waiting to have any service because our emotions are too raw now."

"It was comforting to have Slade with you, I'm sure," I said.

"Yes, it was. He's very, very kind," said Amy.

"Is there anything Rhonda and I can do for you? I understand the five of you plan to make a spa day of it tomorrow."

"I'm looking forward to that," said Amy.

"We all are," Heather said. "We're about to have some refreshments. Won't you join us, Ann?"

"I'm afraid I can't. But tomorrow, Rhonda and I may be able to meet you in the late afternoon. Your time here is going fast, and we hope to spend more time with you."

"That's a plan," said Jane. She walked me to the door. "Thank you for stopping by. I know it means the world to Amy and all of us."

"You five women are more like friends than guests."

Jane gave me a quick hug. "I'll never forget how kind you both were to me. See you tomorrow."

Pleased to know everything was in order at the hotel, I headed home and called Robbie to meet me at the house.

Cindy greeted me at the door when I entered the kitchen. "Hi, sweet girl. Where's Robbie?" I called out to him. "Hi, Robbie! I'm home."

He came from his bedroom to greet me. He'd obviously been crying.

"Hey, what's up?" I asked him, sweeping him into my arms.

"Granny Steph just called. Papa is sick. She asked me to let you know. She sounded scared."

I immediately called Stephanie Willis. She and her husband, Randolph, had been long-time guests at the hotel before they'd become Robbie's adopted grandparents.

"Hi, Stephanie. What's happening? Robbie told me Randolph is sick."

Stephanie let out a long sigh. "Rand has had a cold, which I think has caused pneumonia. He, of course, is declaring he doesn't need to see a doctor and that he's fine, better than yesterday. But he does need to see a doctor."

"I see. What can I do?"

"He adores you, Ann. If you ask him to go to the health clinic, I'm sure he'd do it for you."

"Okay, Robbie and I will come to your condo right now," I said. "I don't like the sound of it."

"Thanks so much. I'm not going to tell him you're on your way. I'll let it be a surprise," said Stephanie.

I ended the call and turned to Robbie. "Come with me to see them. Sometimes, as people get older, they get stubborn about having decisions made for them."

"Is Papa going to die?" Robbie asked, looking as if he might cry.

I hugged him. "I don't believe so. But he needs to be convinced to see a doctor."

When we arrived at Stephanie and Randolph's condo, Stephanie opened the door and bid us to come inside. "Randolph is in the sunroom."

The condo was in a mid-sized building along the beach. The units facing the ocean had one room off the balcony with many windows providing a lot of sunlight. It was a lovely spot to sit among potted plants and relax.

Randolph was lying on a reclining chair when we walked into the room.

Seeing us, he immediately rose in his chair. "What are you doing here?" he asked, smiling.

Robbie hurried over to him. "Papa, you're sick. Granny Steph says so. You gotta go to the doctor."

Randolph, a gray-haired man with well-defined features, glanced at Stephanie. "You're ambushing me?"

"Anything to force you to get help," she said. "We can't lose you to stubbornness."

"Please, Papa," said Robbie.

Randolph sighed. "I suppose I can't say no. Right, Ann?"

"Right," I said. "There's no harm in being seen by a doctor. I can take you to the clinic now. It shouldn't take long at this time of day."

Stephanie clasped her hands. "Thank you so much, everyone!" She helped Randolph out of the chair and hugged him. "We'll all feel better about having you seen. Robbie can stay here with me." She placed a hand on Robbie's shoulder.

"Might as well get it over with," Randolph grumbled to her. He held out his arm. "Ready, Ann?"

At the clinic, I made sure that Randolph and I sat in a secluded area. He filled out forms, and then, when we were called to meet with the doctor, I followed him to the doctor's office.

I listened carefully when the doctor asked Randolph how he was doing.

"I'm fine. Just a little cold," said Randolph.

"His wife and family are concerned that it's more than that," I said.

The doctor began going over Randolph's symptoms and glanced at me.

"We're worried about him having pneumonia. He's had a fever, among other things," I said.

"I see," said the doctor, listening to Randolph's lungs. "Have you had the pneumonia shot?"

Randolph nodded.

"That's positive," the doctor said, "but we'll give you antibiotics to help with this. You're showing the signs of a bacterial infection. I'm also sending home a list of instructions that will be easy to follow, and steps to get you back on track. At your age, we don't want to wait until hospitalization is required."

"Absolutely not," said Randolph, and I couldn't help smiling because I knew how hard he'd fought Stephanie on this.

As we left the clinic with medicine, Randolph thanked me for my help. "It's very gratifying for Stephanie and me to have you, Vaughn, and Robbie, as well as Liz's family in our lives. It has added an important dimension to them. Thank you, my dear."

He gave my arm a little squeeze.

I turned to him. "The pleasure is all ours. I grew up wanting parents and kind, loving grandparents. You and Stephanie are gifts to me and my family."

Randolph quickly turned away, and I could see how moved he was.

In silence, we continued walking to the car.

At home, while Robbie and I were eating a casserole I'd defrosted, Robbie said, "Granny Steph says that we all eventually die."

"Yes. But I'm not expecting either Granny Steph or Papa Willis to die anytime soon. They're both doing well. But someday, they will. Like all of us. But I don't think you have to worry about it."

"I love Granny Steph and Papa," said Robbie.

"I do too," I said. "That's why we must remember to enjoy what time we have with them."

"I still miss Trudy," said Robbie. "She was the best dog."

"Trudy was a special Dachshund. I miss her too," I said.

"Do you think Liz is going to lose her baby? I heard you and her talking about it." Robbie's dark-eyed gaze bore into me.

"I hope not. I don't think she will, but we must let nature take its course. I talked to her earlier today, and she's feeling much better."

"That's great," said Robbie, sounding very grownup.

I gazed at him through misty eyes. Robbie was such an amazing person.

Sitting at our feet, Cindy barked for attention, and the magic of that moment shattered as we focused on the dog who'd replaced Trudy except in our hearts. As she'd shown us, there was enough love to go around.

CHAPTER THIRTEEN

THE NEXT MORNING, RHONDA AND I MET IN OUR OFFICE. After catching one another up on personal news, we discussed hotel issues.

"Manny has the landscaping back in order after the storm. We might want to discuss building a storage unit next to the sundeck," I said.

"Why don't we go down to the beach and look at the area," said Rhonda. "It'll do me good to have a breath of fresh air. Drew is better now, but when he's sick, he clings to me."

"At eight, he still needs a lot of attention. Such a sweet kid."

"Yes, even when he's sick, he's easier to handle than his sister," said Rhonda.

I couldn't help chuckling. Willow, at ten, was very much like her mother.

Rhonda and I left the office and walked to the beach. The minute she stepped onto the sand, Rhonda lifted her arms and gulped in the fresh, salty air.

Beside her, I felt my body lose its tenseness. Relaxed now, I walked toward the water. The beach was strewn with seaweed and other items tossed ashore from the storm. Two of Manny's landscapers were raking up the seaweed in front of the hotel.

The waves washed into shore with a little extra force, still exhibiting signs of the storm, which had now died down. I couldn't stop looking down at the sand to see if I could find a treasure. I was still studying the ground when Rhonda said, "Here comes Brock."

"Well, I see you can take care of your own property but can't be neighborly and assign a couple of your staff to help me," said Brock.

Rhonda placed her hands on her hips and stared at him incredulously. "What is this you're talking about? Are you fucking crazy?"

"I didn't bother telling you about our conversation," I told Rhonda. "It was so ridiculous that I didn't want to rile you up." I turned to Brock. "You already have your answer from both of us now. Just drop the subject."

Brock shook his head. "You'd better be careful what you plan next. I'll be sure to find a reason to block you." He turned on his heel and marched away, his feet pounding the sand like a pouting schoolboy.

"Is he just stupid, or does he enjoy aggravating everyone else?" muttered Rhonda. "He actually asked that of us?"

"Yes, it seems he can't find a landscaping company to work for him after insulting most of the staff at local companies."

"I guess he's just stupid," said Rhonda. "Let's look at the addition we want to make to the sundeck space and pray he doesn't get wind of it."

We walked over to the sundeck. It was a moneymaker for us, but being able to store chairs and other equipment nearby would make it much easier when we wanted it cleared for different functions. And a storage shed would've made it easier to handle chairs and equipment during the last storm.

We had a talented team of architects who usually came up with simple, attractive solutions to any problems we had. Standing next to the sundeck, I could see how we could add a space to the side of the building. Something that wouldn't obstruct the view approaching it from either the hotel or from the beach.

Rhonda and I discussed it and agreed on what we wanted.

"If we're adding to a building we already have, it shouldn't be up to the Neighborhood Association to approve it. A separate building might be different."

"I agree," I said, feeling strongly about it. "We'll quietly get the work done. No fuss, no muss."

"How are our ladies doing?" asked Rhonda, looking at the guesthouse locations.

"Today is a spa day. But this afternoon, we will meet with them for some bubbles. I already told them we would."

"Great. I want to make sure that the death of Amy's ex-husband doesn't overshadow their time here," said Rhonda.

We walked back to the hotel and made sure the library had been restored to its usual décor now that the two days of high tea were over.

"Starting Thanksgiving weekend, we'll have Sunday high teas," said Rhonda. "And then, during our busiest months, we'll offer them both Saturday and Sunday, right?"

"Right, unless the demand is so high that we need to add a day. It's extra work for the kitchen and staff, but people like it, and they make us money."

"Okay, then. What's on the agenda? Do we have a wedding this next weekend?"

"Yes," I said. "I'm a little worried about it because the bride is a famous young actress getting married to her producer boyfriend. Lorraine, who can get along with anyone, has found her to be a bridezilla with a capital B."

"Oh, yes. I remember hearing about her. Someone named Starr Bentley," said Rhonda. "Well, no matter how bad she is, we'll get through it."

"As always," I said. My cell rang, and I picked up the call. *Liz.*

"Hi, Liz. How are you?" I asked, praying for good news.

"I'm fine. Like Dr. Benson told me, nature would take care

of things, and apparently, she decided that I would have this baby. I can't tell you how delighted I am."

"Oh, darling, that's wonderful!" I said, meaning it with my heart. After my talk with Robbie about dying, I couldn't bear it if Liz were to lose the baby.

"I'm still careful about lifting the kids, but things are more normal with me out of bed and active again. I wanted to tell you about the baby and then inform you and Rhonda that Angela and I have a fun idea for the Mother's Pamper Package Program promotion. Next week, we'd like to meet with you."

"That sounds exciting. Just let us know when," I said. "I'll explain it to Rhonda."

I ended the call and embraced Rhonda. "Liz is fine. Dr. Benson doesn't think there's a threat of Liz losing the baby."

"Congratulations. I'm relieved," said Rhonda. "Now, what are our darling daughters up to?"

"They plan to promote the Mother's Pamper Package Program here at the hotel. They want to meet with us next week."

Rhonda grinned. "Sounds like the scare is over. Angela told me how ready they both are to work part-time on publicity for the hotel."

We were always talking about having the girls work for us, but we knew that, realistically, it wouldn't happen until our grandchildren were older and Liz and Angela really would have the time. But we wouldn't complain. It made us happy to see our daughters with their children. Both of us wanted more children, and having so many grandchildren between us was thrilling.

My cell rang. *Vice-President Amelia Swanson.*

"Hello. How are you, Madame Vice-President?"

"I'm right here in Sabal, staying with my sister and Jean-Luc. It was time I came to visit my niece and nephew. I was hoping to see you sometime in the next day or two. Thank you for allowing Slade Hopkins and Henry Watson to stay in one of your guesthouses. It's important that they relax and get some work done for me."

"They both are very pleasant," I said, unwilling to say anything about the women they seemed to be dating.

"I'm glad you think so. They're decent men," said Amelia. "If I can, I'll come to the hotel incognito to thank you in person. I appreciate your help more than you can know. When I think how unhappy my sister was and to see her now with Jean-Luc and her children, I'm grateful for all you've done."

"It's a sweet family. Jean-Luc has never been happier," I said. "I'll thank Rhonda for you and hope to see you."

I ended the call, gave Rhonda the news, and thought about her Henry and Slade. They were likable men, as Amelia had mentioned. But what would happen to those budding relationships when they left the hotel?

"Why do I get the feeling something bad will happen to us if Amelia Swanson is around?" said Rhonda.

"She's not asking us for help, so I don't think you have to worry. She wants to thank us," I said.

"We'll see," said Rhonda. "Now, let's schedule the meeting with our daughters. Our Mother's Pamper Package Program has been suffering, and I think it's time we do something about it."

After talking to Angela and Liz, we set up a luncheon meeting early in the following week to give Rhonda and Will time for a long weekend getaway. It was going to be a quiet time at the hotel. The following week would be Halloween, and we'd be very busy with our new Halloween Weekend Discount Program.

We reviewed our reservation schedule for the next few months and were pleased that there weren't many holes in it.

It was easier to fill the hotel on the weekends, so it was important to offer deals that included mid-week stays. Once cold weather hit the north, it all became easier.

We met with Bernie to discuss the upcoming months, and he agreed that the deals we wanted to market were wise choices.

Toward the end of the afternoon, I said, "It's time to go meet the 'Fab Five' as you call them.

Rhonda grinned. "From what you've told me, I think we have the making of not one, but two matchmaking successes."

"We'll see," I said. "A ten-day vacation doesn't give the participants much time to make anything happen."

But as we walked over to the house, I kept thinking about the relationships that were developing between Slade and Amy, as well as Caro and Henry. The Beach House Hotel was the perfect place for romance.

"I hope the women had a delightful time at the spa. We could use them in some PR info," said Rhonda. "I'll take some pictures on my phone when we get there."

As we walked by the guesthouse where the men were staying, it was quiet.

Rhonda nudged me. "They must be next door."

We knocked on the front door of the "Fab Five's" guesthouse, and Jane came to the door wearing a beach coverup, her skin aglow.

"Hi, Jane. We're here for some bubbles," I said, handing her a bottle of chilled champagne that we'd brought with us.

"Thank you! It's been such a fabulous day at the spa. We're relaxing on the lanai with Slade and Henry. Too bad you didn't bring your bathing suits. We've been enjoying the pool."

"I'm looking forward to spending time with you," said Rhonda graciously.

"Me, too," I said, following Jane out to the lanai. There

wasn't a day in the week or a week in a year that Rhonda would wear a bathing suit in a situation like this.

The other four women cheered when Jane held up the bottle of champagne we'd brought and announced, "More bubbles."

Chuckling, I realized they'd already started with some of their own.

Jane offered us chairs at the table, and we watched as Amy and Slade climbed out of the pool. No doubt about it, Slade was an attractive man, even with a bit of a paunch.

Amy came over to the table and joined us. Slade pulled up a chair beside her.

"It's nice to see you relaxing," said Rhonda.

Amy glanced at Slade. "It's been a few rough days. I couldn't have gotten through it without Slade's help."

"I'm pleased you were able to work out problems together," I said, wondering if their relationship would continue after they left the hotel.

I watched Heather and Lisa sitting on the steps of the pool, chatting. Caro and Henry appeared to be in deep conversation at the far end of the pool.

"I love to see our guests enjoying what we offer them," I said to Jane. "Tell me about the spa. Was it as relaxing as you'd hoped?"

"Even better," said Jane. "And we did agree to have our pictures taken for PR purposes as you'd asked." She poured champagne into two of the plastic tulip glasses we kept at the house.

"Thanks," said Rhonda. "With the beach right here, guests sometimes forget about using our spa."

Caro and Henry came up to the table. "More bubbles?"

"Yes," said Jane. "Let me pour you some of this wine, and then I think we should make a toast to Ann and Rhonda and

The Beach House Hotel."

Heather and Lisa joined us as Jane lifted her glass. "Here's to having the most sensational vacation ever."

"More than we'd hoped for," said Caro, smiling at Henry, who wrapped an arm around her.

I studied them. Caro seemed much younger, freer, and happier than when she arrived. Henry beamed at her, looking every bit like a tennis player with long, muscular limbs and a trim body. Handsome, he had a gentleness about him that was appealing.

We all remained gathered around the table, chatting and enjoying one another's company. Heather, as she usually did, provided us with hors d'oeuvres—crackers, nuts, and a vegetable dip.

We were listening to Slade tell a joke when I noticed a car pull up to the front of the house. A figure emerged from the automobile and started walking toward us.

Surprised, I got up from the table and went to the door, leaving the others laughing at Slade's joke.

"What brings you here?" I asked, my heart pounding at the seriousness of his expression. I could see Amelia sitting in the car.

"Are Henry and Slade here?" he asked. "I must speak to them."

"Come with me." I took his arm and led him to the pool area while another security man quickly checked the house.

When Henry and Slade saw the Secret Service man, the shock on their faces was telling. They straightened as if he'd commanded their attention.

The women were as shocked as they were to then see the vice-president of the United States enter the house with another security man.

"Slade, Henry, you need to come with me now," said

Amelia. "You don't need to pack more than an overnight bag, but we must leave immediately."

"You didn't tell me you knew the vice president," said Caro to Henry in a loud whisper as Amelia stood by. "What else were you keeping from me?"

"No, it's not like that," Henry said. "I'll call you later."

Amelia observed the two of them with obvious fascination. "I'm sorry to interrupt your fun. My apologies to you all. But our time isn't always our own in this business of running the country."

"It was great getting to know all of you," said Slade, addressing the group.

Henry gave a last look at Caro and followed with visible reluctance.

I hurried to the front door to usher them out of the house, wondering what was going on. It had to be some sort of emergency for Amelia to give up time with her sister's family.

When I returned to the lanai, the atmosphere was as if the bubble of fun we all had been enjoying had burst, leaving mere remnants of happiness behind. Caro's eyes filled with tears. "Henry works for the vice president. Don't you think that's worth mentioning? God only knows what else he conveniently forgot to tell me. Maybe that relationship he told me was over is another lie." She covered her face with her hands. "I've been such a fool. I thought I knew him."

Lisa turned to Amy. "Did Slade say anything to you about his job?"

Amy shook her head. "Only that he worked for people in Washington D.C., like a consultant. With everything going on in my life, we no longer talked about it. I'm just as surprised as everyone else."

"It must be an emergency," said Rhonda.

"Yes, Amelia was visiting with family and would never

leave if it wasn't necessary," I added.

"What kind of emergency are we talking about? And why do Henry and Slade have to be part of it?" Caro asked.

"I can only guess that some national crisis has taken place and the men's talents are needed," I said. "I know that Amelia relies on the men to assess a situation and understand the ramifications of any actions taken. They report to her on them."

Jane looked around the group. "We must remember that government secrecy is required in many instances. This has to be one of them. I'm sorry things have ended this way. Who knows when they will return?"

"We most likely will be long gone," said Lisa.

Caro let out a small sob and ran from our group.

"Henry and Caro had planned a romantic dinner alone tonight," explained Lisa.

"It may sound foolish on our part, but I honestly believed Caro had found the perfect man for her," Jane said.

We gathered around the table, sipped our wine, and nibbled on food with less enthusiasm.

A short while later, Caro returned to the group red-eyed.

I wanted to hug her but allowed Jane to direct the conversation. It was easy to see that the other women were used to having her in charge.

"We're not going to let this ruin our vacation," said Jane. "It has been a fantastic time for all of us.

"You're right," said Heather. "And now we've become friends with Ann and Rhonda. Let's enjoy being together."

"It's so charming that the five of you are such close friends," I said. "Thank heavens, I have Rhonda as my best friend."

Rhonda's cheeks flushed with pleasure. "And I've got you, Annie."

I turned to Caro. "I'm sorry to learn that Henry had to leave so abruptly. Will you have a chance to see him again?"

Caro shook her head. "I doubt it. I guess I got caught up in the situation here. I should've known any relationship with him would end, but I couldn't bring myself to think that way."

Heather put her arm around Caro. "Don't say it's over until it is."

"Time will tell," said Amy. "I can't believe I won't at least hear from Slade."

"That's the way to think," said Jane. "Here's to us and all kinds of possibilities."

I lifted my glass with the others and hoped the hotel's magic would rub off on this group of wonderful women.

CHAPTER FOURTEEN

As we left the guesthouse, Rhonda turned to me with a sad shake of her head. "I think Amelia has ruined our chances with these two couples. I hope this trip is very important because you know I hate losing."

"Well, matchmakers can do only so much," I said sympathetically. The truth was nature, not us, made things happen. We might nudge things a little, but that was it.

"It's going to be a busy weekend with a wedding. I'm glad Bernie is relieving us from greeting guests and schmoozing with them occasionally," said Rhonda. "I need a break. I've planned one at the Palm Island Club."

"You and Will really are taking a long weekend off?"

"Yes," said Rhonda, "but the only time we could get is over the Halloween weekend, which means it will be left up to you and the others to oversee it."

"You know we don't mind. You both need to have a break, even a short one. It'll do you both wonders."

"Thanks. We've talked about it for so long I'm not sure I'll believe it when we're finally underway."

"The Palm Island Club is fabulous—great food and a real escape," I said. "Vaughn and I love it."

"We'll see how long Will lasts before he's dying to get back to the office." Rhonda grinned. "I've already bought a sexy outfit to wear."

I laughed and clapped her on the back.

###

The next few days were uneventful. Even the socializing with the five book club women was subdued because no one had heard a word from either Henry or Slade. The Secret Service had directed the hotel to remove their belongings from the guesthouse. Jean-Luc and Amelia's sister, Lindsay, were going to see that their things were returned to them.

When it was time for the women to leave, Rhonda and I gathered around them as they prepared to get into the limo they'd hired to return them to the airport. Tanned and healthy-looking, it was a far different group from the one who'd arrived.

Rhonda and I hugged each woman warmly and smiled at their promises to return one day. Whether or not it ever happened, I'd never forget this special group.

After they left, it was back to business.

As we looked ahead, I was excited about the meeting with Liz and Angela. Liz had told me she was feeling much better, and each time I'd called her, she seemed fine. But I'd be unsettled until she passed her first trimester.

On the morning of our meeting, Rhonda and I decided to do something enjoyable for our daughters and arrange to meet them after they'd enjoyed massages. The spa had a small dining area called the Grotto, where they offered healthy meals , and one could eat in the fluffy robes we provided our customers.

When I called Liz to tell her what we'd planned, she gushed, "Thank you! Thank you! It's just what I need."

I realized one reason I worked so hard was to be able to do things like this for my family and others. "Okay, Rhonda and I will see the two of you when you're through with your massages."

I ended the call and faced Rhonda, who was smiling. "Guess Liz was as excited as Angela, huh?"

"Yes," I said. "I love being able to do this for them. They've been a real help to us in creating PR ideas. They deserve this."

Later, Rhonda and I headed to the spa. Though it was smaller than many, it had grown from a simple operation into something bigger, more luxurious. We'd decided to go for quality instead of quantity. Troy Taylor, the young man who'd helped us with the first one, now owned three spas. With the help of his wife, my first beloved babysitter, Elena, they were doing very well. The friendly, trim, middle-aged receptionist greeted us warmly. "It's so nice to see you both here. Liz and Angela are waiting for you in the Grotto."

"Thank you," we said, and I followed Rhonda into a lovely nook of the building where a few tables were placed on a section of rock floor surrounded by large green potted plants. The sound of a waterfall added to the cozy, tropical feel.

Angie and Liz were sitting at a table drinking glasses of iced water with slices of cucumber added to them.

"Hi, Mom! Hi, Rhonda!" said Liz, jumping to her feet. "I've had such a great morning. Thank you." She hugged us both.

"Yes," said Angela, "it's been delightful."

"It's heartwarming to see you two so relaxed," I said, observing the glow of health on their faces.

"How did Sally Kate do with her kindergarten music program?" Rhonda asked Angela.

Angela laughed. "I'm so sorry you couldn't make it to the show. She was trying very hard to be the star. And she loved the flowers you sent."

"I'm sorry, too, but I couldn't change my doctor's appointment. You know how busy they all are."

"Is everything all right?" asked Liz. She and Rhonda were very close.

"Yes, it was just a routine physical," said Rhonda. "Will and I are going on vacation next weekend. Both of us need a break. My doctor has insisted upon it."

"What about you, Ann?" Angela asked. "Do you and Vaughn get a break too?"

"Yes, we'll take one later," I said. "Right now, it's more important for your father to get away from the office."

Angela frowned. "I've been worried about him. I'm glad you both can take some time off."

"I'm hoping it will be the wake-up call Will needs," said Rhonda.

"Okay, who's hungry?" said Liz, handing out small menus encased in plastic.

It took us only a moment to decide. All four of us wanted the spring green salad with fresh fruit and a yogurt dressing.

"I always feel so healthy when I eat here," said Rhonda, grinning.

"Me, too," said Angela. "But I'll probably have a cookie with the kids for their afternoon snack."

At ease with one another, we all laughed.

After we ate our salads, I dabbed my mouth with a napkin and cleared my throat. "Okay, Angela and Liz, tell us about your PR suggestion."

"I'll begin," said Liz. "We've noticed that the Mother's Pampered Package Program isn't as active as it used to be, and we wanted to come up with a unique way to spur some interest. We decided we had to use real people and real situations for it. Do you remember a young pregnant woman named Jessica Winchester? She participated in the program almost a year ago. Her mother-in-law paid for the three-day pamper program because she was so excited Jessica and her husband were having a baby boy."

"We decided to promote it as a thank you from the husband

and baby for a mother's first year," Angela said. "It would add another layer to the program. Up until now, it's been advertised especially for pregnant women and brand new mothers."

"But what about the young mothers who survive the first year?" said Liz. "That's when it's really important."

Rhonda and I glanced at each other.

"I like it," said Rhonda.

"Go on," I said, becoming excited.

"We got in touch with Jessica Winchester and asked if she and her husband would participate in advertising for the special," said Angela, grinning.

"We told them it would mean a free stay here at the hotel, but they'd have photographers take pictures of them at special times during their stay," added Liz. "What do you think?"

I looked at Rhonda. "I think it's a great way not only to advertise the special program but to showcase the hotel for people in that age group."

"Me, too," said Rhonda. "The rates for that special make it available to young parents who are willing to work around dates for it."

"If it's agreeable to you, we've planned to have them come in early November and stay from a Sunday night to Thursday morning," said Angie.

"Before our Thanksgiving rush," I said.

"Oh, yes," said Liz. "We know how busy that is."

"I think it's great," said Rhonda. "We'll want to see graphics for the program."

"And we need to have some sort of contract drawn up. Bernie can help with that," I said. "If Jessica and her husband are amenable, let's make it an online story on our website."

"That's what we thought we'd do with it," said Angela. "Maybe even put it up on YouTube and Instagram if it comes out right."

"I'm sure glad you two are arranging this. All this online stuff is over my head," said Rhonda. "But I'm proud of both of you."

"Me, too," I said, unable to stop smiling at our daughters. Maybe when the day came for them to take over the hotel, it would be an entirely different way of doing things.

I was still in an upbeat mood when I pulled into my driveway that afternoon. When Cindy didn't come to the door to greet me, my suspicion rose. I hurried through the kitchen and out to the lanai. Observing Vaughn down on the dock, I clapped my hands with joy. Life was so much better with Vaughn at home.

I opened the door to the lanai and headed down the slope of the lawn to greet him.

He sensed my presence, grinned, and then trotted toward me.

When we met, he swept me up in his arms, and I held on tight, never wanting to let him go. After dealing with the ups and downs of running the hotel, I always felt safe in his embrace.

He tilted my chin, and his lips met mine. And I knew from his kiss how happy he was to be here.

"They changed the shooting schedule around, so I have some time off," he said when we finally pulled apart.

"You're in time for our Halloween weekend. Rhonda and Will are taking off for a much-deserved break, but I'll spend as much time with you as I can. How would you like to dress up in costume for dinner on Saturday evening?"

Vaughn let out a sigh and squeezed me tighter. "If you weren't so darn cute, I might say no. But, for you, I'll do it. But only if I have to. I don't want to interfere with the planned festivities by being recognized and forced to sign autographs."

"Absolutely not. That's not fair to you or me," I said.

Cindy jumped around my feet, barking for attention. I picked her up. "Guess she was glad to see you."

Vaughn laughed. "She wiggled so fast she fell. Not that she had far to fall."

I hugged the dog and put her down. "Robbie should be home soon from swim practice. I'd planned just a light dinner, but we can change that to celebrate your being home."

"No, let's keep it simple. Want me to grill up some steaks?"

"Sure. I'll make a salad," I said. Chicken breasts could wait for another night.

"I'll change my clothes, and then we can relax on the lanai." Though temperatures were a little cooler at this time of year, it was still in the low 80s.

"How about a swim?" Vaughn asked.

"You just want to see me in my bikini," I teased.

He laughed. "I've missed being home with you. But, yes, there's that too."

We went into the bedroom together to change.

Glancing at Vaughn as he stripped down to change, I couldn't help smiling. Though we were aging, we worked to keep ourselves healthy for our jobs, and he looked great.

He sensed me looking at him and playfully flexed his arms.

I chuckled and went to give him a hug. Hearing Robbie come into the house, we hurried to get dressed.

"Mom! Where are you?" called Robbie. He stepped into the bedroom as I slid my coverup over my bathing suit.

When he saw Vaughn in his trunks, Robbie grinned and dashed over to him for a hug, crying, "Dad! You're home!"

My heart filled with love for them.

"Are we going out on the boat?" Robbie asked Vaughn.

"Maybe tomorrow. I want to spend some time with you and Mom right here. I'm going to clean up the boat and make sure everything is in order before we take her out."

"Aw, okay," said Robbie.

"How did you do with your swimming?" Vaughn asked him.

Robbie grinned. "The coach expects me to place first at the next meet."

"Great. But even if you don't win, remember to enjoy it," I said.

"I know," groaned Robbie. "I'm hungry. I need a snack after all that swimming."

"Help yourself. Dad is going to grill steaks later, so don't go overboard," I said, amazed at how much my skinny boy could eat, and realized he was about to go through a growth spurt.

While Robbie headed to the kitchen, I grabbed beach towels, filled a pitcher with ice water, and headed to the pool with them and two plastic glasses. It had always been a spot to relax and enjoy one another. I was anxious to know about Vaughn's progress with the movie and what other plans he might have for work. After the holiday rush, I hoped Vaughn and I could take a break. Maybe even go to Paris, as we talked about occasionally.

I sat on the steps of the pool as Vaughn did a few laps. His strong, long arms cut through the water easily, and after completing several laps, he sat next to me.

I offered him ice water, and he eagerly accepted it.

"Ah! That tastes wonderful." Vaughn smiled at me. "And it feels even better to be home with you and Robbie. How is Liz doing? I plan on visiting her and the family tomorrow. I've sent texts back and forth with her, but I want to see that she's okay."

"I understand. Rhonda and I met with Liz and Angela

about a plan they have for a hotel program, and both women looked so relaxed after spending the morning at the spa."

"I spoke to Nell today. She, Clint, Bailey, and Ned want to come for Thanksgiving."

"Fantastic!" I loved Vaughn's daughter, Nell, from the moment I first met her. She and I talked at least once a week, often more. The unusual thing about her was that she and Liz looked alike, as if they could be sisters. They were that close, too.

With the weather in D.C. getting colder, we had a better chance to see them more often.

I floated on my back and looked up and observed puffy clouds of white floating in the darkening sky. Hopefully, tonight, we would enjoy a beautiful sunset.

That night, as we lay in bed, Vaughn and I talked about everything and nothing, catching up with one another as we snuggled together after making love.

"If you want to try to go to Paris in April, I'll mark my schedule. I'm not sure what's coming up after this film. I like the crew and the producer. I'm hoping to get more work from him. But if I don't, I've got other things I can do to support theater programs in Florida."

"Even if a trip to Paris doesn't work out for some reason, it's an exciting thought. The most important thing is being here with you."

"Have I told you lately how much I love you?" Vaughn asked, sweeping a lock of hair behind my ear.

"Not for the last five minutes," I said, chuckling.

CHAPTER FIFTEEN

FRIDAY MORNING, RHONDA WALKED INTO OUR OFFICE AT the hotel. "How's everything? No emergencies?"

I looked up at her and shook my head. "It's safe for you to go, Rhonda. Hurry and leave before you or Will change your mind about having a few days off. We've got everything organized for the weekend. Guests are already arriving. "

Rhonda let out a sigh. "Okay. I can hardly believe it, but I won't see you until Tuesday morning. You'll have to tell me how the Halloween package worked for us."

"I will. I promise." I stood. "Now, go!"

Giggling, Rhonda left the office, and I said a little prayer that this time away would help them both. Especially Will, who'd needed a vacation for a long time. Angela's husband, Reggie, was undoubtedly celebrating that he would be running the financial services office alone, even if it were for such a short time.

A short while later, Lorraine Grace, now married to Reggie's father, Arthur Smythe, entered the office. As our wedding coordinator and social director, Lorraine was a highly valued staff member. We could always count on her creativity and follow-through on details. Aside from that, she was one of the sweetest women I knew.

"How's it going? Did Rhonda get off all right?" she asked me, sitting by my desk.

"Yes, she's both excited and nervous. She hopes this will give Will and her a chance to be together again and have some romantic time."

"I hope it works. Arthur says that Will is a workaholic," said Lorraine. "Heaven knows Arthur is no better, but he worries about their rivalry."

"All because Reggie chose to work with his father-in-law instead of his father. It's a tricky situation."

Lorraine grimaced. "A little hurtful for Arthur. But Will and Reggie work well together, so I think it's all for the best. I see some of our weekend guests have arrived. I've explained that they're welcome to enjoy the hotel, but rooms are usually unavailable until three o'clock."

"Yes, but Rosita promised that her Housekeeping Department would try to have the rooms ready as soon as possible. Each staff member is diligently seeing which rooms are available to clean. They're doubling the teams to do the work."

"Tonight, it's just a welcome cocktail party," said Lorraine. "Tomorrow night is when the work will begin. We're decorating the library for our Halloween guests' special dinner. Of course, we'll add some decorative touches to our main dining room and our lobby."

"What about the menu? I know Jean-Luc doesn't want us to change his dinner menu, but have you come up with some cute items for breakfast and lunch?" I asked.

Lorraine chuckled. "My assistant, Laura, has added some special touches. She put Booberry Muffins on the menu along with Franken Burgers, Haunted Harvest Chowder, Graveyard Greens, Creepy Cobb Salad, Graveyard Grinder, Creepy Club Sandwich, Pumpkin Penne, Skeleton Skewers, and the like."

"Very clever. It adds to the fun of the weekend," I said.

"Yes. For dinner, the waitstaff will wear orange aprons instead of the usual white. And our flower arrangements for the table are all about harvest." Lorraine gave me a playful smile. "I'm even going to wear a Halloween headband, but that's it."

"We're offering a prize for the best-dressed person, which will be perfect. We don't want to overshadow our guests," I said. "Vaughn and I won't wear costumes as we'd agreed earlier." Vaughn was thrilled that he wouldn't have to.

"Exactly what Bernie told us," Lorraine said. "But I bought him an orange handkerchief to wear in his jacket. We'll see if he wears it."

"Our stiff and proper General Manager just might," I said. "Since working for us and marrying Annette, Bernie's brisk manner has softened."

"He's great," said Lorraine. "So fun to tease. A little bit like my husband that way."

"How is he? You both were quite sick with the flu some time ago."

"He's good. Florida has a satisfying lifestyle for him. We both work hard but like to relax together. I've taken up more golf, and having a pool makes it easy to swim and relax there."

"That's great. Even though Rhonda will take the credit for her matchmaking, the two of you are perfect together. Anyone could see that from the beginning."

Lorraine's face broke into a wide smile. "Who knew I'd get a second chance at love?"

Dorothy Stern tapped on the door and entered. "Am I interrupting anything?"

"Not at all," I said. "What can I do to help you?"

"Actually, it's Lorraine I need to talk to about the favors for the Halloween dinner."

"Okay, you two, I've got to talk to Bernie. Anything I need to discuss with him?"

Both women shook their heads.

I rose, and the three of us left the office.

###

When I got home, Vaughn and Robbie were down at the dock working on the sailboat. I changed my clothes and headed down the lawn to join them.

Seeing me, Cindy barked and raced up the slope to greet me. I patted her and sighed with satisfaction as both Vaughn and Robbie looked up and acknowledged me with welcoming smiles. This is what mattered most to me—my family.

"What are you doing?" I asked, coming closer.

"We're testing all the lines and sheets, making sure everything is in order after our summer use," said Vaughn.

"I know the names of all of them," said Robbie proudly.

"This boat is lucky to have the two of you love her so much. Are we going to take a sail this evening?"

Vaughn looked up at the sky. "We can get a quick sail in before dark. I thought about it earlier, and I've already stocked the boat with snacks, hors d'oeuvres, drinks, and a special bottle of red wine."

"You're wonderful," I said as Vaughn wrapped his arms around me.

"Yay! Dad said I can be captain," said Robbie.

"He's ready." Vaughn ruffled Robbie's dark locks.

We put a life jacket on Cindy and climbed aboard.

"Toss the docking line aboard, matey," said Robbie, laughing as he spoke.

"Aye, Captain," Vaughn responded, waiting on the dock until Cindy and I were settled in the cockpit and Robbie had the engine running.

"Okay, all aboard," said Robbie.

Vaughn tossed the docking line into the cockpit and stepped aboard just as the boat pulled away from the dock.

Vaughn sat in the cockpit beside me and wrapped an arm around my shoulders. "Ah, this is it. Relaxing on the water." Though he remained in his seat, Vaughn kept an eye on

Robbie's movements to make sure all was how it should be. But I knew from the looks he gave me that he had something important to tell me when the moment was right.

Once we motored out of the inlet and into the Gulf waters, Robbie faced the boat into the wind, and he and Vaughn raised the mainsail and then the jib.

I held onto the wheel while they did.

Robbie hurried back to me and took the helm so he could lay off the wind onto a port tack and the sails could fill. Vaughn sheeted in the jib and then checked the mainsail's trim to eliminate any luffing. Then Robbie cut the engine.

We surged forward and heeled a bit as the wind pushed the sailboat ahead.

I was always thrilled with these first moments of quiet, hearing nothing but the sound of the boat cutting through the water with a soft hissing sound. The seagulls and terns flying in circles above us filled the air with their cries, which were carried in the wind.

I let out a long breath of satisfaction and turned to Vaughn, who gave me a wink to acknowledge how I felt. For him, sailing was the most gratifying way to relax.

I gazed at Robbie behind the wheel, a skinny but muscled boy who would soon become a man. Where had the time gone? I couldn't help but think of my life with his father, who'd turned out to be someone I didn't know, someone whose only unselfish act toward me was to give me Liz and then Robbie. My children meant more to me than even the best memory of our marriage.

"I've got something to tell you," Vaughn murmured. "I'm thinking of doing more stints with the soap opera. It seems *The Sins of the Children* is going to go back to the time when I, as the mayor, was in love with Lily Dorio. It would be just a few episodes, but they think it's important for their continuing storyline. What do you think?"

I let out a sigh that came from deep inside me. "You know how I feel about Lily Dorio. But I trust you to do the work required and then to come home. Will they promise to stop any rumors of an affair between the two of you?"

"They said they would. But it could happen with today's social media being out of control. I'll tell them no if you want me to."

"Oh, Vaughn, I can't let this stop your career. It's a big part of who you are, and I respect that."

He smiled at me. "Thank you."

"Hey, Galley Cook, how about a can of soda?" teased Robbie, and I left bad memories of Lily Dorio behind as I went below to get Robbie's drink.

I pushed aside my concerns about Vaughn's work and concentrated on work at the hotel. I promised I'd be present for the Halloween cocktail party in the library. About forty people were participating in this private event of cocktails and dinner. Later, the lanai would be open to all guests for after-dinner drinks and live music. Vaughn would join me for that.

Annette was acting as hostess and stood by the door greeting people as they arrived, handing them each a goodie bag filled with sweets and small gifts from local businesses, including our spa.

"Hi, Ann. It seems like a fun crowd," said Annette, wearing a headband and holding a small witch's hat. It was the perfect touch to her black slacks and tasteful top.

I gazed at the guests filling the room. Costumes were optional, but most people in the room wore a costume or added a Halloween touch to their outfits.

"Lorraine organized a Halloween treasure hunt for guests

this afternoon, which was a big hit with this crowd, who had to walk to various places in town." Annette shook her head. "I don't know how she manages to pull off things like this."

"She's a treasure of her own," I said, looking up as Lorraine joined us, wearing black slacks and a burnt-orange top accented with a black bead necklace and a black cat pendant.

"Hello," said Lorraine. "It looks like another successful party is underway."

"I'm keeping my eye on the young woman in the corner by the bar," said Annette. "She's had quite a bit to drink. Her date doesn't seem to be aware of it."

"Or he's trying to ignore it," said Lorraine, sounding like she'd been in this situation before.

"We don't want anything bad to happen to her or one of the other guests," I said. "I'm going to make my rounds and then leave to go home. I'll be back with Vaughn for the party on the lanai."

"Thanks, Ann." Lorraine smiled at me. "I know it's a pain to spend the time, but having you and Rhonda welcome our guests makes them feel important."

"That's one reason we do it," I said. "Truthfully, we decided when we opened the hotel that we would treat our guests as if they were being welcomed in our very own home. It's kept a lot of people coming back. We might be a small operation, but we are and always will be very special."

"Exactly right," said Annette.

I left them to speak individually to our guests. I was always interested in who was in the hotel and what brought them here. I'd learned a lot about others and, in the process, a lot about myself.

Most of this crowd was younger than usual, and I was delighted to see it. We were a high-end property, but we welcomed people of all ages.

I was talking to a young man when the woman who'd been drinking came over to us.

"Happy Halloween," I said, smiling at her.

She looked at me with glassy eyes, put an arm around the man's neck, and threw up on him.

His look of shock was replaced by one of anger. "I'm sorry about the mess," he said. "I'll take her back to our room."

Annette hurried over to us to help, and a bartender brought several black napkins and water over to the spot on the carpet and started to clean up.

I moved away to give him space and went to another area to talk to our other guests, who, fortunately, hadn't noticed the incident. I knew Bernie would address the situation in our staff meeting on Monday morning. We trained our bartenders to cut off people who were under the influence of too much alcohol.

Lorraine sidled up next to me and said softly, "I'm sorry. I'll speak to my staff about situations like these."

"It happens, but we must be careful," I said. I turned to the couple I'd been talking to and introduced Lorraine to them.

By the time people were seated for dinner, I'd spoken to almost everyone. I watched as the first course of shrimp cocktail was served, and then I escaped to go back home. I'd return later with Vaughn.

Vaughn and I walked onto the lanai for the after-dinner party, which was open to all guests. The fact that he was well-known as an actor always made it awkward at first, but guests soon realized that he was with me, and he wanted to enjoy himself—that, and the fact that they had to sign a privacy agreement.

A well-known singer in the area, Kitty Carwell, was at the

microphone while another well-known musician, Dee Morton, played the piano. They were often paired up, and the result was fabulous light jazz.

Kitty sang a slow number, and several couples started to dance.

Vaughn held out his hand. "Shall we?"

I smiled at him and rose. He was a graceful dancer, and together we moved well. As he held me in his arms, I felt my memories carried back to when I first met him, when we first held hands, and now, as I did then, I knew that I was so lucky to have found him.

"Are you thinking back to the beach with me when we first met?" he whispered in my ear.

I chuckled. He knew me so well.

"I am, too," he said, his voice soft and affectionate. "And you're as beautiful now as you were then, those few years ago."

I sighed happily. I felt we'd always somehow been together, just waiting to meet again.

As we left the dance floor, Lorraine and her husband, Arthur Smythe, Reggie's father, joined us.

"The evening weather couldn't be better," said Lorraine, still holding hands with Arthur.

"The guests certainly seem to be enjoying it," I replied. "Shall we make our rounds? Then, I want to go home."

"Sure," said Lorraine. "There's someone I want you to talk to. They have friends who are getting married, and she wants to recommend The Beach House Hotel."

While Vaughn and Arthur stood talking, we headed into the crowd.

CHAPTER SIXTEEN

I WAS STILL LAZING IN BED THE NEXT MORNING WHEN Rhonda called. "Ann, I'm at the hospital with Will. Can you come?"

"Absolutely. What's wrong?"

"They're still testing him. We're at the NCH Heart Institute." Rhonda sounded as if she were about to cry.

"I'm on my way," I said, jumping out of bed.

Minutes later, I was dressed and explained to Vaughn what was going on.

"Keep me informed," said Vaughn, looking worried. He and Will had always gotten along well. Though Will wasn't a sailor, he and Vaughn played golf together whenever they could.

"Tell Robbie I'm sorry I won't be able to make his swim meet. Remember, Stephanie and Randolph will be there. If you want to invite them to dinner, I'm all for it. But it's your time at home, so do what you want."

"Okay, thanks. I'll let you know how things go," he said, kissing me.

I used to like to have things properly planned, but with the uncertainty of our job requirements, I'd learned long ago to roll with whatever happened.

I found Rhonda in the emergency waiting room, pacing the floor. I hurried over to her and gave her a hug. "Any news?"

She nodded. "They're scheduling him for stent surgery."

"Were you able to see him?" I asked her.

"Yes, but he was already on his way into surgery, so I could only say how much I loved him." Rhonda's voice shook. "They said the blockage was pretty severe."

"What brought this on?" I asked her.

Rhonda sighed. "The first night we were there, we had dinner and relaxed in our cabin. We agreed not to talk about business until we both had a chance to unwind. The next day, we read and relaxed on the beach, took naps, and ..." Rhonda's cheeks turned red.

"And dinner?" I asked before Rhonda could say anything more.

"We ate an early dinner and kept it fairly light."

"When did you get him here?"

I woke up around six this morning, and Will was out of bed, just sitting in a chair. I knew something was wrong. After speaking to him, I called the front desk for help. We made the water crossing and got here to the hospital in record time. They said the surgery usually takes from thirty minutes to two hours."

Rhonda continued, "The hotel keeps a doctor on call, and when he heard the symptoms, he said to get him here as fast as we could. A staff member from the hotel accompanied us."

"That was important, something we've done at our hotel. But it's probably time for another training session for our staff."

"Yes, I thought of that too," said Rhonda.

"What can I do to help? Would it relieve your mind if I checked you out of the hotel and packed up your things?" I asked.

"Yes, maybe you can go there with me after the procedure," said Rhonda. "For now, I need you here."

I hugged her. "Not a problem. How about breakfast? Can I

get you some coffee and something to eat?"

Rhonda rubbed her stomach. "Actually, yes. I've been too upset to think about food, but it sounds good now that you're here. We can go to the surgical waiting room. That's supposed to be more comfortable than here."

"Okay, let's go." I took her arm, and we followed directions to the elevator and up to the surgical floor.

When we went into the ladies' room, Rhonda looked in the mirror at herself. "I didn't realize I was such a mess. I just threw on the same caftan I wore yesterday and didn't realize I'd spilled something on it. I've got a comb in my purse."

"You're fine. No one cares. I'll leave you to this and get us some coffee and something to eat." I left Rhonda and went to the café, where I bought coffee and two sweet rolls.

"You're an angel," said Rhonda when I handed her a cup of coffee and a cinnamon treat and then sat down beside her.

"The sweet rolls can't compare to Consuela's, but it's something to eat," I said.

"Nothing can compare to hers," said Rhonda before taking a sip of coffee.

After we finished eating, I sat quietly with Rhonda. I knew her well enough to know when she was ready to talk, she would.

"I'm not sure what's going on with Will. He said he'd discuss a concern with me and then backed off, telling me it was nothing for me to worry about, that he'd taken care of it."

"Will's so competent; I'm certain that if he told you not to worry, he meant it," I said.

Rhonda gave me a thoughtful look. "But I don't think it's something that just happened. He's been unusually quiet about work. Not that he can share any confidential information. Angela said Reggie's been preoccupied lately. Maybe it has something to do with that."

"Both Will and Reggie are straightforward men. If there were anything either you or Angela should know, they would tell you."

"You're right," admitted Rhonda. "Having Arthur in town with all his big New York clients has been unsettling. I get the male ego thing, but it's something more than that."

"Getting back to Will's health, have you been given information about what happens after this procedure?" I asked her.

She handed me a bunch of pamphlets. "They wanted me to be prepared for the time we go home. They told me they'd probably keep Will overnight to make sure everything went well, but that I should be prepared for lifestyle changes he should make and possible emotions and feelings that he might be dealing with."

"I can understand that. Will must slow down now or face worse consequences," I said.

"I think this wake-up call is going to be difficult for him," said Rhonda, frowning. "He already feels threatened by Arthur. And Reggie's eagerness to take over and run the office is another issue. Will's not ready for retirement, but he'll have to make some changes."

I got up from my chair and moved around. I remembered when Vaughn's plane went down over Alaska and the awful emptiness that I'd felt at the thought of his not being found. I glanced back at the worried look on Rhonda's face, how her shoulders had hunched up, and vowed to be with her every step of the way. The months ahead wouldn't be easy.

"This couldn't come at a worse time," said Rhonda. "The holidays are coming up and then high season. I want to be able to support you as much as possible with the hotel, but I have to make sure Will is all right and able to take care of himself."

I sat down beside her. "I agree. The hotel staff does a

wonderful job for us. We'll handle it."

"On the other hand, I can't babysit Will every day. He'd kill me, or I'd kill myself," said Rhonda.

"We'll do this together like we always do."

As we were talking, a man wearing green surgical clothes approached. "Mrs. Grayson?"

Rhonda glanced at me and stood. "That's me, and this is my friend, Ann Sanders. Is everything all right? How did my husband do?"

"Hi, I'm Dr. Hamblin. He did just fine. He's had three stents put in, which was one more than we'd initially thought we'd need. We'll keep him overnight to make sure everything's fine, and then tomorrow, before he's released, we'll have him meet with one of the rehab nurses. I'd like you to be present for that, as he will need to change his diet and lifestyle."

"I'd love to be there for that," said Rhonda. "I've been a voice in the wilderness, so to speak, for a long time. I need someone else to tell him what he can and can't do."

"I agree it will be helpful for that meeting. You should be aware of the emotional impact something like this can have on a patient. Your husband might become very frustrated with the changes required."

"I'm sure of that, so I think we need to be in this meeting together. May I see him now?"

"Yes, he's in the recovery room. He'll remain there for a short time, and then he'll be moved to our cardiac unit. Ask the nurses on that floor, and they can tell you when he's brought there. It should be any time now."

"Thank you, Doctor. Thank you so much," said Rhonda, trying not to cry.

I put my arm around her.

The doctor gave a little bob of his head to both of us and moved away.

#

After Rhonda had seen Will and spent a few minutes with him, she and I headed to the Palm Island Club. This small resort was unique in that it was situated on a small island off the shore of Sabal and was approached by a short boat ride. It was a favorite relaxing spot for Vaughn and me.

The clubhouse was a light-stained log cabin-style building which, from the outside, didn't reflect the elegance inside. In addition to guest rooms in the main building, ten cabins lined the sandy beach, offering upscale privacy to those inside. Vaughn loved lying on the beach in front of one and then using the small private pool behind to cool off. We'd spent many happy hours there.

While Rhonda checked out, I began packing up for her. It was easy to fold things up. Staying at the resort meant wearing nothing very dressy, just simple clothes for an easy getaway.

As I closed Will's suitcase, Rhonda walked into the bedroom. "Have you done my stuff yet? I don't want to leave behind the sexy nightgown I bought for the occasion." Rhonda's smile disappeared, and she plopped down onto the king-size bed. "Oh, Annie. What's going to happen to Will and me? Will he be the same as before, or will he think he's too old or fragile to make love like we used to?"

"Those are questions that the rehab center can answer. I'm sure other women have wondered the same thing. I remember a guest of ours talking about how great it was for her husband to recover from stent surgery and that it positively changed his life. He felt so much better, more alive."

Rhonda sighed. "I won't worry about it now. The important thing is that Will has been saved from a heart attack. With all the stress he's been under, it's a wonder he hasn't dropped dead."

"He's always been a strong, active man. I don't see that

changing," I said.

Rhonda got to her feet. "I don't want to add to my worries by thinking of things that might never happen, right?"

"Right," I said. "We're going to get through this and enjoy the life we have."

"Sounds like a plan to me. Now, where's that sexy nightgown?"

When I finally got to the hotel to see what was happening there, Lorraine's staff was changing out the Halloween decorations in the dining room to our usual fall ones. I looked in on the library. All was in order there. On the lanai, the only trace of Halloween was a black cat made of stone sitting among the landscaping by the bar.

Lorraine hurried over to me. "Bernie told me Will was in the hospital. Is everything okay?"

I filled her in and said, "Rhonda's going to be busy at home for the next few weeks trying to make him slow down."

"If it helps, we don't have a wedding for a couple of weeks, not until the Saturday following Thanksgiving." Lorraine shook her head. "These men and their work. I swear Arthur is a workaholic. But that works for us, with me and my job here."

"I know things have been a little tense for Will for some time," I said. "Hopefully, this episode with his heart will help him understand that he must change his work pattern."

"I hope so, too." Lorraine placed a hand on my arm. "I'm so glad Arthur and Vaughn could spend time together at the party last night."

"It's important because we're all part of what I call 'my hotel family.' Speaking of family, I will ask the front desk about departures and arrivals, and then I'm going home. See you at the staff meeting tomorrow morning."

"Okay. I won't be far behind," said Lorraine. "Arthur is going to take me out on the golf course. I'm getting better."

"Have fun," I said , leaving her thinking how lucky Rhonda and I were to have found her to handle weddings and social activities for the hotel.

"How's Will?" Vaughn asked as I approached him, sitting on the lanai reading.

I sat down on the couch next to him and let out a sigh. "I hope this will be a wake-up call for him. He had three stents put in, demonstrating how serious his situation was. He will have to participate in a rehab program to help him change his diet and lifestyle habits."

"Why was he so driven with his business?" Vaughn said. "I understand the stock market is always changing, and he must keep up with it, but I can't imagine he has to work all the time. Especially with Reggie there to help him."

"Reggie is his partner and a very capable financial advisor," I said. "I think Will feels a little threatened by him, and he's definitely threatened by Arthur, who deals with much bigger accounts."

"Funny you should mention that," said Vaughn. "Arthur spoke to me about a special offering he has available. Supposedly a big money maker. I agreed to look at some of the material he wants to send me."

"I'm not surprised he was pushing work on you. Lorraine and I were talking this morning, and she said Arthur is a workaholic, but it works out well for the two of them."

"Well, I'm glad you and I can work out times to be together with our crazy schedules," said Vaughn. He drew me to him and kissed me on the forehead. "Let's keep it that way."

I snuggled up against him. "I think we should."

CHAPTER SEVENTEEN

AFTER OUR MONDAY MORNING STAFF MEETING, I CALLED Rhonda and filled her in on the discussion. "We're supposed to meet with Angela and Liz regarding the young couple arriving tomorrow for the Mothers' Pamper Package Program. Are you able to do it?"

"Yes. Why don't the three of you come here for lunch? Rita can fix some sandwiches and a salad. I'll get Will ready. He's been sleeping in the downstairs bedroom. The doctor wants him to take it easy for a couple of weeks. He's not allowed to drive for a while, which is difficult for him. And, yes, like I was warned at the rehabilitation center, he's grumpy as hell."

"Well, then, the sight of Angie and Liz should cheer him up," I said, pleased to think it might be helpful. Will Grayson wasn't typically a grumpy guy.

Right after noon, we entered Rhonda's house, prepared to help Rhonda and Will. With Willow and Drew in school, it was quiet when we walked into the kitchen.

Liz and I waited there while Angela went to find her stepfather, a man she adored.

In moments, Angela and Rhonda entered the kitchen together. "Why don't we meet here? Rita is feeding Will, introducing him to a grilled chicken salad instead of his usual burger for lunch."

"Oh, oh. I bet that isn't going well," I said, glancing at Rhonda, who made a face and shook her head.

"I had no idea he was having that kind of lunch until he was forced to confess it at the Heart Healthy rehab center program we were assigned." Rhonda signaled us to come over to the table. "Have a seat. I've made some salad plates for us."

"How's Reggie doing with all the changes?" I asked Angela quietly.

"He loves being in charge, but he also misses having Will there. Their clients love Will for his honesty, even when they want to do something he doesn't approve of. Reggie has a younger clientele who are more willing to try new things."

Rhonda carried the salad plates over to us, poured glasses of iced tea, and took a seat at the table. She raised her glass of tea. "Here's to us!"

"Yes!" said Liz, and we all raised our glasses. "I want this new project to turn out well for us."

"Okay, tell us what you've arranged," I said.

"Mr. and Mrs. Winchester, Jessica, and Ryan will arrive tomorrow. When she was pregnant with her little boy about a year ago, she participated in our new Mother's Pamper Package and loved it."

"We want those women to come back with their husbands for a Couples Pamper Package, and she and her husband seem like a perfect choice to test it," said Angela. "They have agreed to be photographed at different stages so we can feature them in our brochure. In exchange, we will cover their stay and any legitimate expenses they might have while here."

"We figure featuring both programs on our new brochure and doing some online advertising campaigns doubles the draw," said Liz.

Rhonda and I glanced at one another. "Tomorrow, we'll greet Jessica and Ryan, welcome them to the hotel, and show them to their room, which will have a welcome basket, fresh flowers, bottled water, and cookies," said Angela.

"Our hotel terry robes will be placed on top of the king-size bed, along with spa slippers for each," Liz said, a glow of excitement on her face. "We'll close the door, leaving them to their privacy. From there, we'll have shots of them having breakfast in bed, lounging on the beach, dining in the dining room, and being at the spa and the pool. It's a small property but very special."

"And we'll definitely show them watching the sunset together. It should all be very romantic. A time to get back some of those moments after being sleepless for months," said Angela.

"You've talked to Jessica and Ryan about all of this?" I asked.

"Oh, yes. She sounded desperate for this, which will give an added dimension to the publicity shots," said Liz. "Will the two of you be able to greet them when they arrive? They should get here around eleven o'clock."

"I'll make it," said Rhonda with fresh determination, and I wondered how one of the sweetest marriages I knew was holding up.

We discussed some other special PR projects Angela and Liz were handling and then spent time catching up on family news.

By the time we left, I was ready to go home. Robbie had invited his best friend, Brett, to go sailing with us and have a light supper. It was a beautiful, sunny day, and I wanted to share it with them and Vaughn.

I hugged each of our girls and turned to Rhonda. "Let me know what I can do to help."

"Thanks. I complained about not having enough time alone with Will. Now, it might be too much togetherness. But I'm very thankful to have him around and am grateful the doctors seemed to have done an excellent job with him. All I have to do is convince Will that changing his ways won't be so bad, and he can finally relax."

I hugged her and left, worrying about how much Will would be able to relax after working so hard since Arthur had breezed into town.

Later, sailing with Vaughn and the boys, I began to let go of my worries. When I was under sail, they seemed weightless. Time would help Will heal, and his friends would step in to help in other ways.

The boys, best friends since they were toddlers, were fun to watch as they took turns sailing the boat under Vaughn's watchful gaze.

We kept our conversation light. It was always interesting to hear what the boys had to say about their activities and school. Normally, it wasn't easy to get more than one-word responses from either one of them. I'd learned not to ask questions that could be answered with just a word or two. Open-ended questions were much more successful.

The wind picked up as storm clouds appeared on the horizon.

"We'd better head back now," Vaughn said to the boys. "Announce when you're coming about, and we'll take it from there."

"Okay, here it goes. Coming about!" said Robbie.

Sitting in the cockpit, I ducked my head as the boom swung and the boat headed back to shore.

Vaughn helped Robbie trim the sails, and with a stronger wind, we moved fast across the water.

Later, after motoring into the inlet, Vaughn and the boys washed the boat down and tidied it before closing and locking the cabin.

While they worked, Cindy and I hurried out of the rain.

Inside, I put away the food from our picnic and prepared to serve the chocolate cake we hadn't had time to eat aboard the boat. No one could resist any dessert I brought home from the hotel. Not even me.

CHAPTER EIGHTEEN

THE NEXT MORNING, IT SEEMED LIKE OLD TIMES AS Rhonda and I went down the hotel's front steps to greet Jessica and Ryan Winchester for their Pampered Couples Package.

Gazing at the two of them emerging from the limousine, I noticed how strained their smiles were, and I hoped they hadn't just had a fight. We couldn't back away from it now with so many people lined up to help make this PR move happen.

"Hello, welcome to The Beach House Hotel," I said to Ryan, offering my hand as Rhonda spoke to Jessica.

I was aware of the cameras focused on us.

"Thanks for having us," Ryan said, glancing at Jessica. "This is the first time we've ever been away from the baby. My mother is babysitting."

Rhonda and I exchanged places, and I had a chance to speak to Jessica. "We hope you enjoy your special stay with us," I said. "Your husband said this is your first time away. Let's make this a special time for you both."

Jessica smiled. "We'll try to." She lowered her voice. "His mother is staying with the baby. It was supposed to be my mother, but she got sick and couldn't do it."

"I'm sure Ryan's mother will do a satisfactory job. I can promise you that being a grandparent is an honor. I have three of my own and another on its way."

Jessica studied me for a moment. "Do you love them all the same? I'm worried that if we have another baby, he or she will never be as loved as our baby boy, Wade."

"With love, there's always room for more," I said and turned as Ryan joined us.

"Let's go see our room," he said to Jessica.

"Liz Bowen and Angela Smythe, your hostesses for the next couple of days, are waiting for you in the lobby," I said.

We walked into the hotel together, and Rhonda and I stayed behind as Liz and Angela came forward to greet them.

Watching our daughters take on our roles as greeters, I felt a pang. The day would come when they would do those jobs permanently. But not until we all were ready.

I glanced at Rhonda and could see from her expression that she felt the same sense of loss at handing the hotel over to our girls.

"I'm not ready to give it up, are you?" she asked.

"Not yet." I hugged her, and we stood there as observers.

Much later, before I left the hotel, I went to see Lorraine's assistant, Laura. "You're trailing our Pamper Program couple, aren't you?"

"Oh, yes. Liz and Angela made it clear they wanted someone from the hotel to be aware of what was happening with Jessica and Ryan at all times and to notify them if there were any problems. They seemed a little worried about it."

"If this works, it could become an important campaign. We'd be doubling the original Mother's Pamper Program by following it up and connecting it with a couples program."

"It's a great idea," said Laura. She frowned. "So far, not much is happening. Ryan has been wandering around the property alone."

"I'll walk by their room," I said. "If I hear them inside, I'll see if they need anything and be able to assess the situation."

"That would be great," said Laura. "I'm to stay in the background. Jessica and Ryan are supposed to have their picture taken at dinner tonight. Liz said she'd be here, but we want to be sure they're up to doing it."

"Okay, I'll see if they're around. If not, I'll leave to go home."

I left Laura's office and wandered down the hallway to the bridal suite where we'd placed Jessica and Ryan. At the end of a first-floor corridor, the suite had an oversized patio and plenty of privacy created by lush landscaping. It was a perfect place for brides, honeymoon couples, and romantic getaways.

When I approached the room, I could hear Jessica's voice. "You don't understand. You haven't even tried to understand what I'm going through since the baby and I came home from the hospital."

I glanced around. The corridor was empty, so no one would've heard this.

Hoping I wouldn't be making a mistake, I tapped on the door. Ryan answered the door.

"Hi," he said as Jessica walked outside to the patio.

"I just wanted to know how things are going. Are you two going to be able to be photographed at dinner tonight?"

"Come on inside," said Ryan. "We're trying to adjust to time away from our usual routines."

Jessica approached us. "Ryan thinks I'm here to play with him. I do want to do things with him and follow our contract, but he doesn't understand that for the last ten months, I haven't had a decent night's sleep. He thinks because he doesn't hear the baby cry at night or can leave for work the next day that I should be able to handle it myself. This afternoon, all I wanted to do was sleep. I'm so damn tired."

"But that's how it always is," grumped Ryan.

Trying not to panic, I said, "Why don't we talk about it?"

"We haven't been able to talk about it at home with either set of parents. They're so excited about becoming grandparents until it's time for them to babysit. Then it's a different story," said Jessica. "My parents live four hours away, but Ryan's parents are in town. However, they're usually too busy to help."

Ryan frowned at us. "She's right. We don't have the help we thought we'd have. But I'm under too much pressure at work to do much at home."

"What about the weekends?" I asked.

"I take care of our baby Wade for two hours on Saturday afternoon," said Ryan.

"While he naps," Jessica said with an edge to her voice.

"Do you have a friend you can exchange babysitting with?" I asked Jessica.

"Yes, but she and her baby are always sick," said Jessica. She turned to Ryan. "I'm sorry. I know you wanted this to be a big weekend for us."

Thinking of how our plan was failing, I said quietly. "We can make this weekend work. Let's start now. Will you trust me enough to come to the beach with me for a short while?"

Jessica and Ryan glanced at one another.

"Okay," said Jessica. "What do we have to do?"

"Just come with me. It's very pleasant. You won't need your sandals or shoes."

We left the patio and walked out to the beach.

Jessica stood a moment, feeling the soft sand on her feet. She looked up and smiled at Ryan. "It's so warm and soft."

Wearing Bermuda shorts and a T-shirt, Ryan lifted his arms, embracing the sunlight. "I love the smell of the water."

"Let's just walk down to the water," I said. "I've found a special way to relax. My husband and I do it to reconnect when he's home from a business trip."

As the three of us walked toward the water, I kept watch on the couple from the corner of my eye. Ryan reached for Jessica's arm to steady her, and after a tense couple of seconds, she allowed him to lead her.

At the water's edge, I pointed out the little footprints of the sandpipers and sanderlings who ran along the frothy edge looking for food. Above us, seagulls and terns circled and cried out, looking magical as they swooped and swirled.

"Step into the water," I said. "Feel the sand curl around your ankles as the waves come in and return in a pattern as old as time. Then hold hands and close your eyes."

Jessica and Ryan did as I suggested.

I stood nearby and spoke softly. "Let the sun warm you and the water anchor you to the earth. Listen to the sounds of the birds and people around you and allow them to block out all other thoughts except for a feeling of gratefulness to be here in this place at this time."

I remained quiet for several minutes and then said, "When you're ready, open your eyes and look at one another."

I felt relief at the looks they were giving each other.

"When I'm stressed, overworked, and tired, I practice this exercise. It works for me every time. And when my daughter, Liz, whom you've met, is feeling the need to feel grounded, she and I come together for this."

"I hear she has triplets," said Jessica. "How does she do it?"

"She has a lot of help, but she and her husband work out a schedule where they each have time alone with the kids and away from them. It seems to work."

Jessica gazed at the water thoughtfully.

Ryan said, "Okay, let's take a walk on the beach. Thanks, Mrs. Sanders, for your help."

"I hope you have a delicious dinner," I said, pleased to see the change in them. "I'm sure I'll see you tomorrow."

I was relaxing at home with Vaughn after he'd returned from a sail when my cell phone rang. *Laura.*

"Hi, there. What can I do for you?" I asked.

"I didn't want to disturb Liz or Angela. I know how busy they are with their kids. But we have a problem with our special couple."

"What's happened?" I asked, alarmed.

"They're both drunk. They were too drunk to have their photos taken in the dining room. I've helped them order room service to get some food into them. But it's too late for them to go to the dining room."

I frowned. "Did they tell you what's going on? Why did they do this? They seemed fine this afternoon."

Laura hesitated and then said, "Jessica accused Ryan of getting her drunk so they would have sex."

"Oh, I see. Well, let's make sure they get plenty of food tonight so they're ready for the spa tomorrow morning. You'd better tell Liz and Angela what has happened. They need to be prepared."

"Will do," said Laura.

"I'll let Rhonda know. Maybe we can come up with a plan for how we all can get Jessica and Ryan through the next couple of days."

After hanging up with Laura, I called Rhonda and told her what had happened.

"I thought the girls had vetted couples carefully," said Rhonda.

"They had four couples fill out their questionnaire and felt Jessica and Ryan presented the best chances for a cute story," I said.

"We've spent money arranging photographers and lining up staff to help. We'd better make this work. It's hard to coordinate everyone," said Rhonda. "I'll meet you at the spa tomorrow morning."

"How are things going with Will?" I asked.

"He's an unhappy camper," said Rhonda. "But he was very glad to see Vaughn earlier today."

"Oh, great. I haven't had a chance to talk to Vaughn about it. I love that they're friends.

"Yeah, me too," said Rhonda. "See you tomorrow."

As I ended the call, Vaughn looked up from the book he was reading. "What's going on?"

I filled him in on the situation and then said, "Will is very glad you went to see him today. How is he?"

"Both grateful to be alive and miserable at being held back from working." Vaughn made a face. "It was odd, but he asked if I was doing business with Arthur. I knew that Will was competing against him, and I didn't know how to respond. But when I told him that I wasn't, Will seemed very pleased. I'm not sure what that's all about, but I'm staying out of it."

"That situation is getting out of hand. I hope that if Will stays out of the office long enough, his need to compete with Arthur will end. I know it worries Rhonda."

"The thing is that Arthur wants to speak to me about an investment he has. But I'm going to call him and tell him I'm not interested."

"I think that's best," I said. "Will and Rhonda are our closest friends."

"I'll try to visit Will again," said Vaughn. "The poor guy is bored silly, and it's only been a short time."

"Yes, anything to keep him busy away from the office." I leaned over and kissed Vaughn. "You're such a wonderful man. I love having you around."

"About that," said Vaughn. "I'm waiting to hear from the producers when we start shooting the movie again. So far, it's been a smooth operation, but something always comes up. I'm thinking I won't have much more time here."

"Before you must go, will you take a walk on the beach with me?"

"Always," he said. "I love those moments with you."

CHAPTER NINETEEN

THE NEXT MORNING, I WENT TO THE HOTEL EARLY TO
check on Jessica and Ryan. They were scheduled to be filmed
having breakfast in bed, and I wanted to be sure they were
ready.

When I knocked on the door, Ryan answered it, looking a
bit ragged. "Morning. We're running a little late, but Jessica
and I will be ready for the photoshoot."

"Great. Liz and Angela will be here shortly and will help
you prepare." I glanced into the room and realized the
housekeeping department might need to be called into action.

Disappointed but leaving it to Liz and Angela, I went into
the kitchen for my morning coffee.

Consuela was there pulling sweet rolls out of the oven. My
heart warmed with love. She was the epitome of who I'd
always wanted as a mother instead of the stern grandmother
who raised me. She was kind and loving.

Consuela turned, saw me, and smiled.

As soon as she set down the hot pan on the counter, I went
over to her and hugged her.

"Everything okay, *querida*?" Consuela asked.

"Yes, I'm just so grateful you've always been part of my
hotel family."

She cupped my cheek with her hand. "*Te amo.*"

I hugged her again. "Me, too."

I grabbed my cup of coffee, accepted a sweet roll from
Consuela, and headed into the office.

I was still looking through email on my computer when

Rhonda came into the office carrying a cup of coffee and a plate with a sweet roll.

"Morning!" I said, noting the scowl on her face.

"Hopefully, these will brighten my day," she grumbled. "It feels as if I have added a toddler to the family. I'm trying to be patient with Will, but he's difficult to live with right now."

"It must be hard for both of you," I said. "I don't think you'll do any relaxing here. Let me tell you about my morning visit to our special, romantic couple."

"Uh-oh. What's wrong now?"

I told her about the condition of the couple and their hotel room. "I think it's best to let Liz and Angela handle it."

"Yeah, me too, because right now, I'd want to shake them both. They signed contracts to do this."

"We'll see about things at the spa, but again, leave it up to Liz and Angela to handle any problems."

"Probably that's best. Let's go out to the beach and look at the progress on building our storage shed by the sunset deck. With Brock's interference, it took forever to get the permit."

"We certainly don't want the shed to be obvious, so there was no reason for him to make such a fuss."

Rhonda's eyes narrowed. "It's all about his ego."

As soon as she finished her coffee and we'd talked about any issue that might need our attention, we rose and went outside to take a walk on the beach. It was always an excellent place to talk and plan about the future.

The day was warm and humid, and the threat of rain was present when we walked out to the beach. The waves rolled into shore and back again and had a darker tone to them without the glare of sunlight. But I still thought they were beautiful as they met the shore with a timeless rhythm. The salty hiss left behind as they pulled away was something you could hear only in quiet moments.

I was standing at the water's edge, eyes closed, when an annoying voice said, "Well, the two ladies I wanted to talk to."

Feeling as if I'd been smacked awake, I turned to face Brock.

"What do you want, Brock?" growled Rhonda, and I knew she was trying to hold in her temper. She had no patience for him, especially when he'd given us such a hard time with a building permit.

"I just needed to see when your new construction will be complete," said Brock.

"The construction is complete," I said. "As to the exterior finish, we're working on that now. It is to be stained the same color as the sunset deck structure so it will be less obvious. But as you no doubt know, the structure can't be seen from the beach, so the rest isn't your concern."

"Mind your own business," said Rhonda, putting her hands on her hips. Aware she was about to lose all control, I grabbed her arm and all but dragged her away from him.

Brock must have been aware of how close Rhonda was to unleashing her frustration on him, and he said nothing as we left.

"Thanks, Annie," said Rhonda. "All I needed was another whining person near me to make me want to explode."

"Let's walk for a while. We can talk as we do," I said. Rhonda might be blunt and outspoken, but she wasn't usually this volatile. Things must be stressful at home.

During our conversation, I said, "Vaughn is going to visit Will again."

"That would be great," said Rhonda. "Will was going to talk to me about some of his work while we were away, but we never got to have that conversation. So, right now, any diversion would be helpful to him. He's stewing about something."

I told her how Will had asked Vaughn if he'd had any dealings with Arthur and was pleased he hadn't.

Rhonda shook her head. "I don't know what is going on between Will and Arthur, but it's tearing Will apart. I think it might have something to do with their competition for Reggie's attention."

"It's hard to have family work for you," I said.

"Will and Reggie are close, and they've been working well together. I think that's what is driving Arthur crazy. I think he wants Reggie to know he could be making a lot more money working for him."

"Has Angela mentioned the tension between them to you?" I asked.

"Yes. She told Reggie that she trusted him to do what was right and that while she'd support the choices he made, she didn't want to become embroiled in any disagreements. While she recognizes that Arthur is Reggie's father, Will is hers."

"That's so smart of her," I said. "But if anything serious is going on, Reggie owes it to her to fill her in."

"Right," said Rhonda. "Reggie continues to show his loyalty to both Angela and Will, so I don't think the problem is there."

The longer we walked, the calmer we both felt.

"Let's see the storage shed. The stain should've settled by now."

Rhonda shook her head. "Brock needs to be careful with how he conducts himself. I'm not the only one who'd like to see him disappear."

As we approached the sunset deck, I hoped Liz and Angela would be able to have their special couple photographed.

Pleased with the progress on the building, we left the beach to see if any new problems had arisen.

###

Later that morning, we met Angela and Liz at the spa. Jessica and Ryan were already getting massages.

"How are things going?" Rhonda asked.

"They were in pretty rough shape this morning," I said.

"We got them through the breakfast in bed scene after a private talk with Jessica, who's been going through some emotional times," said Angela.

"Oh?"

Angela made a face. "Ryan wants another baby, and Jessica doesn't. That's why she was so mad at him for getting her drunk. She thinks he did it on purpose to get her pregnant."

Rhonda and I exchanged worried looks.

"I tried talking to Jessica myself for a while, simply as a friend," said Liz.

"Be careful what you say," I said, and Rhonda nodded in agreement.

"None of us is a professional," said Rhonda.

The photographer arrived, interrupting us. "You wanted some shots of his and hers massages?"

"Yes," said Liz. She looked at her watch. "We should be able to do that now."

Later that afternoon, Angela called to invite us to a high tea session with Jessica and Ryan.

"We thought since it was cloudy, we'd do a beach shot tomorrow. We're still aiming to do a sunset shot. Then tomorrow will be a relaxing day for Jessica and Ryan before they have to return home."

"Smart idea," I told Angela. "Are Dorothy and her friends joining you for tea?"

"Yes," she said. "They've agreed to be photographed in the background."

"Perfect," I said and handed the phone over to her mother.

"Be sure the waitress is dressed in costume," said Rhonda. "We talked about it at our meeting." Rhonda listened and then laughed. "Okay, okay. I know you girls have control of the project. Thanks."

Rhonda ended the call and turned to me, looking downhearted. "I guess our daughters don't need us to tell them what to do."

"Rhonda, we want them to do more and more projects for us. Right?"

"I'm a mess," admitted Rhonda. "I have too much going on at home and have to learn to give up some control at the hotel."

"Just give it time," I said. "Now, let's see about the high-tea photo session."

We left for the library, where a section had been decorated for high tea with pink tablecloths on two tables for four. Each table held a small crystal bud vase holding a single pink rose. Special flower-patterned white dishes and teacups sat at each place.

Jessica and Ryan had changed into clothes suitable for the occasion, with Ryan in pants and a golf shirt and Jessica in a sundress.

The visit to the spa and, perhaps, Liz's talk with Jessica seemed to put them in a relaxed, almost loving mood.

"Hello," I said. "I hope you enjoy our high tea."

"It looks delicious," said Jessica. "I can't wait to taste the treats."

"Me, too, even though those sandwiches sure are small," said Ryan, chuckling.

I laughed. "Have as many as you want after the photographer is through."

Dorothy approached us. "Hello, I'm Dorothy Stern. I

volunteer here at the hotel. My friends and I are delighted to be here for the photoshoot. We'll be in the background."

Rhonda made the introductions, and then Angela came over to us. "We thought we'd have some shots of the two of you alone from different angles. It'll be easy like the rest. Just follow the instructions from the photographer."

I left them to join Dorothy and three of her friends, who were loyal customers of the hotel restaurants.

"Thanks for joining us, ladies. I have no idea how long this will take, but enjoy yourselves."

"Oh, we will," said one of Dorothy's friends, beaming as two multi-layered trays filled with tempting treats were placed in front of them.

Rhonda and I didn't stay long. We'd put our daughters in charge and owed them their privacy.

As we walked toward our offices, Rhonda stopped me. "Let's see what treats are in the kitchen. Everything looked delicious. Maybe I'll take one home to Will. That might sweeten him up. Anything is worth a try. Right?"

I grinned. "Maybe then, he'll tell you what's bothering him.

CHAPTER TWENTY

AN HOUR LATER, RHONDA AND I HEADED TO THE library, anxious to see how the high tea photoshoot had gone.

When we walked into the room, we were surprised to see Angela and Liz sitting with Jessica and Ryan, laughing and talking.

Liz got to her feet when she saw us. "Come on over. We've been talking about some of the early days at the hotel."

"No wild tales," said Rhonda, pulling up a chair and sitting with the group.

I joined them. "Those were some pretty tough days."

Jessica shook her head. "I don't know how you did all of it when you had young children at home."

I laughed. "Talk about being busy with young children at home. Together, Liz and Angela have six children under the age of ten. And another on the way."

Jessica's eyes rounded. She turned to Liz. "I knew you have triplets, but I didn't know you were having another baby."

Liz chuckled. "It was a big surprise. I wasn't sure I could handle it. But I have a supportive family and friends."

Jessica shook her head. "I know I couldn't do anything like that. One baby is so much work."

Liz studied her. "Tell you what. Why don't you and Ryan come to my house? You can meet the kids and see how it works for us."

Jessica and Ryan exchanged glances, and then Jessica said, "Okay, thanks."

"Angela and her husband, Reggie, are close friends with me

and my husband, Chad, so it works well to get together. Sometimes, we end up having dinner as one big group."

"It's special," said Angela, smiling. "We let our kids play together and have some adult time to socialize."

"Mom? Rhonda? Want to join us?" asked Liz.

"I'm sorry I won't be able to this time," said Rhonda, getting to her feet. "In fact, I'd better go. The kids will be getting home from their school activities, and I need to keep an eye on Will."

"I'm delighted to be invited," I said. "I haven't seen the Ts in some time, and I need a GeeGee fix." I faced Jessica. "My son, Robbie, has swim practice, so he'll be late getting home from school."

Later, I was sitting on the patio at Liz's house, watching Chad and Ryan toss a ball back and forth. The triplets, laughing and shouting with glee, raced back and forth between them, trying to get the ball.

Angela had called to say they'd be a bit late, so while Liz was fussing in the kitchen, I had a chance to talk to Jessica alone.

"You mentioned that your baby, Wade, is ten months old. Is he an active child?"

Jessica's lips curved. "Yes, he's not walking yet, but he's into everything. I can't leave him for a second. It's exhausting. Ryan wants more children, but I don't see how I can handle it."

"I wanted more children before and after Liz's arrival, but it didn't happen. I've always been sad about it. Having my grandchildren means the world to me. Does Ryan help you with the baby?"

"Not really," said Jessica. "I mean, he's gone for the day

and is tired when he gets home."

"He looks like he's enjoying the kids now," I said. Ryan was on all fours on the grass, giving Noah a "horsey ride."

"Yeah, well, he isn't that cooperative about changing diapers," grumbled Jessica.

"Does he ever do that?" I asked.

"Sometimes, but I'm left alone all day to take care of everything," said Jessica. " Ryan's ready for more children. But even the thought of it is exhausting to me. I was hoping that by coming here for the promo opportunity, he would see that we don't need more kids; we just need to reconnect with each other."

"Have you talked to a professional about this? It might help to understand one another's point of view."

"Maybe that would help," said Jessica, sighing. "Look at Ryan now."

Ryan had both girls on his back now, prancing around on the grass. Nearby, Chad held Noah upside down by his feet as Noah shrieked joyfully.

Liz joined us. As soon as she sat down, all three kids came running over to her. "Can we have a juice?" Olivia asked. "We're all thirsty."

Liz started to stand.

"Sit tight. I've got it," said Chad. "C'mon, kids. Inside."

The look of surprise on Jessica's face was matched by Ryan's.

"Is that how it always is?" asked Jessica. "Chad helps?"

"Yes. I may be the mom, but Chad is the dad and has to share in the care of the kids. Otherwise, he's not doing his job."

We sat quietly until the kids burst outside, each holding a sippy cup. "Remember what I told you," Chad said to them. "No running around while you're drinking your juice. You might choke on it. Sit and drink it."

The three children ran over to their wooden table and sat in chairs at it.

"They're so well-behaved. How do you do it?" Jessica asked Liz.

"You haven't seen them fighting or fussing or how they act when they're over-tired. All of that happens. But even at a young age, we had rules for them. We had to," said Liz.

"They're still mischievous and get into trouble because they're so curious, but they do listen when you talk to them," I said.

"Yeah, my mom was like that. Easygoing but with rules. I've got three brothers, and she made us all mind. I want to give Wade brothers." Ryan paused. "Or sisters."

"I didn't like growing up without a sibling," said Liz. She turned to me. "But I've always known you wanted more."

"I was thrilled to have you," I said softly, glancing at Jessica, who kept watching the triplets.

"We're here!" said Angela as three children dashed past us and onto the lawn. The oldest, Evan, carried a soccer ball. The two little girls, Sally and Izzy, held dolls.

Reggie appeared carrying a tray with cheese and crackers. "Hello, everyone; I'm Reggie, Angela's husband." He set down the tray and shook hands with Ryan and Jessica as they were introduced.

Sitting beside me, he said, "Nice to see you, Ann."

"How are you? You must be busy handling the office alone." I studied the dark circles beneath his eyes.

"I'm busy, but it's fine. I'm just worried about Will. Something's off with him. I know he's been wrestling with a personal problem, but he refuses to talk to me about it."

Liz interrupted the conversation. "Okay, what can we get to drink for everyone? We have lemonade, iced tea, and a light white wine. And water, of course."

After drinks were taken care of, I hoped to resume my conversation with Reggie, but he rose to talk to Chad.

Olivia and Emma ran over to me and climbed into my lap together. After juggling their bodies into comfortable positions, I hugged them both and began talking softly to them. We did a three-way patty cake game, with all of us laughing.

In minutes, they scrambled out of my lap to go back to the yard to play with the other kids.

"That was quick," said Jessica.

"Oh, yes, but I'll take every moment I can with them. How about Wade? Does he have a playtime with a grandparent?"

Jessica made a face. "My mother-in-law lives in town. But we don't get along that well. And when she babysits Wade, she won't follow my directions."

"Really? What are they?"

"Well, I keep Wade on a special schedule. He needs to go to bed at a certain time, wake up at a given time, and eat on my schedule. My mother-in-law likes to do her own thing with him."

"Has that hurt him in any way?" I asked.

Jessica's cheeks grew pink. "Now, you're sounding like Ryan. He's not hurt; he's just thrown off his schedule, which is one that I follow online. They say you must stick to it if you're going to raise a secure child. Believe me, I want to do everything right for our baby."

"I'm sure you do, but didn't Ryan say he had three brothers? That was a lot for his mother to handle. I'm sure she has some tricks of her own for keeping her children happy and secure."

Jessica let out a long sigh. "My mother is too busy with all her social activities to see the children often. Of course, she lives four hours away, so a visit would usually mean an overnight stay, which neither of us wants."

Chad cleared his throat. "Time for a toast. It's always interesting to meet new people. Jessica and Ryan, we're glad you came to The Beach House Hotel. Thanks for being part of the promo program Liz and Angela are running."

"Thanks for having us," said Ryan. "I remember how excited Jessica was when she came for the new mother's program."

"Yes, I'm delighted to be back at the hotel. It's such a beautiful place." She glanced at Ryan. "Magical, almost."

After a while, I left to get home for Robbie. But as I drove away, I hoped some of the magic of the hotel would stay with Jessica and Ryan. They had a lot to work out.

The next morning, I told Rhonda what Reggie had said about Will having some sort of problem he wouldn't discuss.

"It's the same situation for me. I won't press him on it until he's feeling better and stronger. But it's a conversation that will have to happen sometime."

Angela and Liz arrived to give us a status report on the promo project.

"It's going well. The sunset and dinner shots were fabulous. We'll take one photo at the beach this afternoon, and that's all," said Angela.

"I don't know what you said to Jessica, Mom, but she told me she enjoyed her talk with you," said Liz.

"Just girl talk," I said. "It was very sweet of you two to entertain them yesterday afternoon. I think it's something they'll always remember."

"Ryan told Chad he hoped it would make a difference in some choices they had to make," Liz said.

"Yes, it was helpful for Jessica and Ryan to see what it was like having so many children around," said Angela. "Jessica told me she wasn't so afraid to loosen her schedule."

"We're going to do some work in Dorothy's empty office and then go home," said Liz.

"Thanks for all you're doing," said Rhonda. "I'm sure you don't need any guidance from us."

Angela chuckled and went over to Rhonda to give her a hug. "How's Dad today?"

"Better," said Rhonda. "It's just a matter of time before he's more like himself. Or so they tell me."

"Okay. Talk to you tomorrow after Jessica and Ryan leave."

After Angela and Liz left, Rhonda and I exchanged looks of satisfaction.

"I did good. Right?" said Rhonda.

"Yes. And me, too. I wanted to ask a million questions, but I didn't."

Rhonda and I gave one another high fives.

CHAPTER TWENTY-ONE

AFTER JESSICA AND RYAN'S VISIT, RHONDA AND I SPENT some time with our daughters, who were developing an online PR program and an update to our website. Even though our hotel did very well, we were always looking for ways to keep our guest rooms full. If the weather worked against us, there was nothing we could do about gray, rainy, cold days. However, we could find ways to provide guests with alternatives to sunning on the beach.

Thanksgiving was looming. The day itself was the busiest of the year in our restaurant, providing several shifts of guests with the delicious food for which the hotel was known. I loved the excitement of the day, which also signaled the approach of the Christmas holidays. This year, I was especially excited to have Vaughn's daughter, Nell, and her family stay with us for Thanksgiving.

Nell and I had a close relationship. We'd connected when we first met. Maybe because she looked so much like Liz and was just as charming. She'd encouraged Vaughn to date me. Married now and with two children, she and her husband, Clint, lived in Washington, D.C.

I was working with Dorothy on last-minute seating arrangements for Thanksgiving when I received a call from Nell telling me she and her family wouldn't be able to come for the holiday because all four of them were sick.

"I'm so disappointed," I said, feeling let down. "You know how I love to spend time with you."

"I do, but I can't expose you or the rest of the family to

whatever we have. We're watching the kids carefully for pneumonia. They're that sick."

"Oh, no! Poor things. I hope they and you all feel better. It sounds terrible. You sound awful."

"I don't remember when I last felt this sick," said Nell. "I know you'll be busy. Think of us when you're at the hotel with all that wonderful food."

"I wish there were a way to send some to you," I said. "Let's plan a visit at a later time. I hope you all feel better. Please keep in touch. Love you."

"Love you too, Ann," said Nell, coughing.

Disheartened, I ended the call.

"Nell isn't coming?" asked Dorothy. "Such a shame."

"It is because it's one time of year we can share a holiday," I said. "I'll text Vaughn. He's on his way home."

Dorothy pointed to the chart she'd updated. "I think this will do it."

I looked at the new arrangement. "It's great that we have this online. We can make changes if we have to."

"It's too late for more requests, isn't it?" Dorothy said.

"Yes, we can't accept any reservations for that day. We're slightly overbooked as it is."

"I remember when it wasn't so complicated. But then, the hotel was new. Now, people called weeks in advance for a reservation for dinner."

"Thanks for your help in confirming the reservations."

"You know I love helping you girls," said Dorothy. Her eyes behind thick glasses gleamed at me. "Poor Rhonda. She'll be glad to get back to a full routine. How is her husband doing?"

"His health problems are under control. But he's still wrestling with issues at work. That's why Rhonda is keeping a careful eye on him. He's allowed to go back to the office for half-days only."

"I hope things calm down for her," said Dorothy. "She's such a special person; she's so generous and caring."

"Yes," I said, trying to hide my worry. She and I knew something was going on with Will, but he still wouldn't talk about it. He said time would take care of it.

Later, I was working on financial projections for the holiday season when I received a call from Caro Corbin.

"Why, hello! How are you? Have you recovered from your bubbly vacation here with your friends?"

Caro laughed. "Yes and no. We all had a fabulous time. And we're all planning to come back sooner than we thought." There was a ring of excitement in her voice. "I know this will sound absurd to you, but Henry and I have been together as much as we could these past several weeks, and we've decided to get married. Crazy, huh?"

I clapped a hand to my chest. They were such special people, and I knew about her ex and how he used to put her down constantly. We'd all seen the connection between Caro and Henry from the beginning.

"Well?"

"You two together are perfect." I warmed up at the images of them here at the hotel.

"We want to get married at The Beach House Hotel. Do you think we could do it on Sunday after Thanksgiving? I know it's a busy time for you, and I suspect Saturday is out. It will be a simple, private wedding for only sixteen people, and ..."

"Hold on," I said, stopping her. "We do have a wedding on Saturday. But we could do your small wedding that Sunday evening. What accommodations do you need?"

"Are the houses available that weekend? Caro asked.

"Let me see. Hmmm. One house is available that Friday, the other not until Saturday."

"Please hold. I'm texting Henry now. I'm in Pennsylvania

packing up. Henry is at our new apartment in D.C."

"Yes! He says we'll take both of them. One on Friday and one on Saturday. But he asks if we can have them through Tuesday. The parents are making room reservations on their own."

"That's fine. I'll notify the reservations department. Send a deposit right away to confirm the houses. Would you prefer me to send that information to Henry?"

"That would be great." She gave me his phone number and then gushed, "Oh, Ann. It was such a lucky day when the book club decided to come to The Beach House Hotel. It's such a magical place."

"It was a lucky day for us, too. So, all five of you will be here?"

"Yes. They'll come with me on Friday. My parents, Henry, his parents and brother, and Slade will come later." She giggled. "I feel like I'm in the middle of a fairytale. Henry is everything I've always wanted in a man. I don't know how I went so wrong the first time."

"This is very sudden, but I'm sure you've both thought it through," I said.

"We've talked and talked about everything from our favorite books to how I feel about his Dachshund, Duke. It's all so fantastic. First, to be taken in by the book club, the youngest in the group, and secondly, to meet a man and know right away that he was the one I've been waiting for my whole life."

"And Henry feels the same way?" I couldn't help asking.

"Yes. He was engaged once but couldn't go through with it. But now, he's ready, with me, and doesn't want to wait. I don't either."

I heard the catch in Caro's voice and felt a sting of tears. It was a true love story. I couldn't wait to tell Rhonda.

###

On my way home, I drove to Rhonda's house. We were so used to seeing each other every day that it seemed only natural for me to go out of my way to visit her.

When I rang the doorbell, Willow answered. Her face lit up at the sight of me, and I wrapped my arms around her. "Hi, Sweetie. Where's Mom?"

"In the kitchen. Rita's not here, and Mom has to make after-school snacks for us," said Willow, taking my hand and leading me inside.

"Hi, Auntie Ann," said Drew, grinning at me. "We're having peanut butter treats. Do you want one?"

I looked at the toasted bread cut into squares and topped with peanut butter. "No, thank you."

Rhonda laughed. "They were easy to do. I've been making some of Will's favorite foods, so I haven't time to fuss now."

I walked over to the stove, lifted the lid on a pot, and inhaled the garlicky tomato sauce.

"Delicious. Your mom's recipe?"

"I'm trying to be careful about what food we eat, but Will is so thin I want to give him some home cooking. What can I get you?"

"How about a cup of coffee? It's been quite a day. I've got some exciting news for you."

After Rhonda made sure the kids were set, we took our coffee to her upstairs sitting area. It was a favorite spot in her house where we could have some privacy.

"So, how are things going with Will?"

Rhonda frowned. "He said he was going to talk with Reggie about something that's been bothering him. I don't know what it is, but I was glad to hear he's talking to someone about it. How about you? You said you've got exciting news?"

"Guess what! Caro, who is part of the book club group, and

Henry are getting married at the hotel on Sunday after Thanksgiving."

"Wow! It didn't take them long to let the hotel and our matchmaking skills go to work," said Rhonda.

We looked at one another and laughed.

"Seriously, they've been talking every day and being with one another as often as possible," I said. "Henry was engaged once before and backed out, but now he's ready and doesn't want to wait. He also knows what a miserable time Caro had with her ex. That must have something to do with wanting their relationship to be stable.

"They're perfect together," said Rhonda, reinforcing my feelings. "You could see how well-matched they were. I'm surprised it's happening so quickly. But then, after knowing what her friend, Amy, went through with her ex-husband being found dead and all of us realizing how short life is, I get it. No reason to wait."

"I think it's doubly sweet they want to be married here. Henry is renting both houses that weekend. One on Friday and the other on Saturday. Caro says it's going to involve only sixteen people. So, it will be small and simple."

"Is it going to be on the beach? The weather is a little unpredictable then," said Rhonda.

"I don't know. Caro is talking to Lorraine about it now, I suspect."

Rhonda took a sip of coffee and smiled at me. "You know, Annie, we've always thought of the hotel as our home, allowing people to stay and enjoy it. I've wanted our guests to find the same happiness we've found here with each other and with our families. I think that's why I enjoy matchmaking so much. It just seems right. Ya know?"

"I do. Caro called the hotel magical, and I think of it that way too."

"Let's keep that feeling going," said Rhonda. She lifted her coffee cup, and I clinked mine against hers.

That night, Robbie and I had just finished dinner when Vaughn walked into the kitchen.

Cindy, Robbie, and I all raced to him to greet him.

Vaughn set down his suitcase and hugged Robbie, patted Cindy, and then drew me into his arms. "Mmm. I've missed you." He noticed Robbie standing by. "Missed all of you."

"What can I get you to eat?" I asked. "We have the fixings for Elena's tacos. Want some?"

"Sounds delicious." He reached into the refrigerator for a cold beer and opened it. "It always seems like a long flight home. What's happening here?"

"I'll let Robbie tell you about school and everything while I put together a meal for you. I thought you'd be home later."

"I was able to catch an earlier flight and grabbed at the chance to do so. We wrapped up shooting, and I don't have any commitments away until sometime early next year."

"Perfect," I said and listened as Robbie and Vaughn talked while Cindy continued to wriggle with happiness at Vaughn's feet.

It always felt better with Vaughn at home.

Later, after Robbie was settled for the night, Vaughn and I were able to show each other how much it meant to have him here.

CHAPTER TWENTY-TWO

THE NEXT MORNING, WHEN RHONDA WALKED INTO THE office, I saw fresh circles under her eyes, and then I looked more closely. Her eyes were swollen.

I got to my feet. "Rhonda! Are you all right? What's happened?"

"It's Will and Reggie. Will did as he told me he would and talked to Reggie about something at work. Now, neither Reggie nor Angela is talking to either one of us. I don't know what the conversation was, and Will wouldn't tell me."

I hugged her and then sat down. "This doesn't sound like any of them. What could it be?"

Rhonda shook her head. "All I know is my family is about to explode, and I can't do anything about it. I'm furious with the three of them. I'm glad the holiday week is here. I need to keep busy."

"Okay, then. Dorothy and I have taken care of the confirmations for Thanksgiving dinner and upgraded the seating chart."

"There will be more changes tomorrow, but it's smart to have it organized for the moment."

I'd just printed out the room reservations for the weekend to show Rhonda when Lorraine stumbled into the office. "Arthur has been arrested."

Rhonda and I shot up out of our seats.

I held onto Lorraine as she collapsed into a chair, crying. "What's wrong? How can we help?"

"It has something to do with his office and a financial

offering. As they took him away, Arthur told me not to talk to anyone about it, but I had to come to you. I don't know what's going on, but I need to be there for him."

Rhonda and I glanced at one another.

"That's it," said Rhonda. "Oh my God. It all makes sense. I have to call Will."

"I'll stay right here with Lorraine," I said.

"I'll use Dorothy's office," said Rhonda.

After Rhonda left, I turned to Lorraine. "Have you called a lawyer?"

"Oh, yes. Arthur gave me the name of one in Tampa. He was warned this might happen and tried to handle it before it became a bigger issue."

"Where is Arthur now?" I asked.

"He's at the county jail. He told me he won't be there long." She cupped her hands over her face. "It was so embarrassing to have policemen drive up to our door and take him away."

"I'm sure," I said.

Rhonda returned. "I just talked to Will. I'm sorry, but I can't be involved with this. Lorraine, I hope things turn out right for you and wish you all the best." Her eyes glistened with tears; Rhonda hugged Lorraine. "I have to go home. This is ripping my family apart."

"I'll come as soon as I can," I told Rhonda. Facing Lorraine, I said, "I'm going to call our lawyer, Mike Torson. You may need one for your own purposes."

"I know Mike. I'll call him myself. Thanks for your help, Ann. I don't want to make trouble for anyone."

I got up and hugged her. "Lorraine, you're part of the hotel family. We're here for you. After talking to Mike, please let me know what we can do to help you."

As soon as she left the office, I called Vaughn.

He listened as I told him what had happened and then said,

"I'm glad I didn't take Arthur up on going in on a special deal one of his friends was offering."

"You knew something was wrong?" I asked, shocked.

"No, I have my own financial advisor and don't use anyone else. It's best that way. I trust him completely."

"I wonder if this is what was bothering Will. Rhonda had to go home. I told her I'd come as soon as I could. Hopefully, I'll find out more information. Talk to you later." I ended the call and gathered my things. I'd talk to Bernie first, and then I'd go see Rhonda.

When I drove up to Rhonda's house, I noticed that Will's car was not in its usual place in the driveway beside Rhonda's gray Mercedes.

When I knocked on the door, Rita answered it. "Come in, Annie. Rhonda's waiting for you upstairs in the sitting area. I'll bring coffee."

"Thank you. How is she?"

Rita shook her head. "She's crying hard."

I raced upstairs. Rhonda was a softie who didn't hide her feelings, but she didn't cry often. It must be bad.

When I walked into the sitting area, Rhonda was staring out the window, wiping her face with a tissue.

"Rhonda, I'm here," I said softly.

She turned and got to her feet.

I stepped forward and embraced her, feeling her shoulders shake.

"It's going to be all right, whatever it is," I said. "Tell me what's going on."

"Everything is messed up. Neither Angela nor Reggie will take my call. Will told me not to go to their house and that I was to stay out of it."

"What is going on? Tell me what you know."

"Like you, I know Arthur got arrested. Will told me it was insider trading."

"And Angela and Reggie?"

"Reggie thinks Will told the authorities about it. And he told Angela she's not to talk to either one of us until it was proven otherwise." Rhonda dabbed at her eyes and drew a deep, shaky breath. "Angela and I have never not spoken to one another, even through difficult times."

"Maybe there are legal implications in conversing with them," I said, handing her a fresh tissue from a box nearby.

"That's what I have to believe," said Rhonda. "You know how competitive Will and Arthur have been. Truthfully, Arthur loved to brag about his big New York City clients and all the connections he had. It bugged Will no end."

"I've always thought Arthur was jealous of the relationship that Will and Reggie have," I said.

"I'm sure that's part of it. But now, Reggie is turning against Will, saying he believes Arthur and that the person who notified the SEC was Will."

"That doesn't sound like Will," I said. "If he thought something was wrong, he'd say so to Arthur's face."

"I think that's what Will has been hiding for the past few months." Rhonda clapped a hand to her chest. "My God! He almost died from a heart attack, keeping the suspicions to himself. Wait until I tell Angela that."

I put my hand on her shoulder. "Remember, you can't talk to Angela until things get straightened out."

Rhonda nodded. "I need to talk to Will. Will you come to the office with me?"

"Yes," I said. Will wasn't supposed to be under any undue stress. This was the worst—having his reputation and his business possibly ruined by something out of his control.

#

Rhonda and I entered the office of Grayson and Smythe to find it quiet. We didn't see Reggie anywhere, and we found Will closed away in his office. He looked up through the glass partition of his office wall and stared at us.

I waited outside while Rhonda hurried to Will and put her arms around him. After a few minutes, Rhonda gestured to me to come inside the office.

She and I sat in chairs in front of Will's desk.

"We need to know what exactly is happening," said Rhonda. "You said something about insider trading."

Will cleared his throat. "To put it simply, insider trading involves trading in a public company's stock or other securities by someone with non-public, material information about the company. Insider transactions are legal if the insider makes a trade and reports it to the Securities and Exchange Commission, but insider trading is illegal when the material information is still non-public. That's where Arthur went wrong."

"So, he bought stock in a company before it became public?" I asked. "It seems so simple. Why would he do it?"

"To make money, of course. But I think he wanted to show me up. He's been trying to get Reggie to leave the company, telling him he'd make more money working with his group out of New York where the big money is."

"But there are plenty of millionaires right here in Florida," I said.

"Including your wife," said Rhonda. "I trust you with my money because I know you and respect how honest and hardworking you are, just like every other client of yours."

"You are every bit as successful as Arthur," I said, furious that Will was being blamed for any part of this. "How can you prove you didn't report the situation?"

"That's all part of the investigation. Arthur was brought in for questioning. I suspect the SEC has already built a case against him and the others involved."

Rhonda gazed at Will with such love that I looked away. "Will, darling, is this what has been bothering you these past few months? You've been so worried, so upset about work."

Will looked down at his desk and lifted his face, looking miserable. "Arthur and I have been competing—no question about it. But when I told Reggie that he couldn't mention this opportunity to any client of ours, he got angry and told me I had to stop competing with his father. Things have been tense between us since then."

"Shouldn't Reggie be grateful to you now?" asked Rhonda.

"Like I said, he thinks I may have let it slip about it being a bad deal. The trade would've been legal if made after the forthcoming sale of the company was made public. It's as simple as that."

"There must be a reason Arthur went ahead with it," I said. "He's an honest man."

"True, but he got greedy," said Will. "His friend at the company gave Arthur secret information about the forthcoming sale of it and promised it would be made public on a certain date. But the so-called friend didn't follow through. Arthur bought enough shares to indicate obvious knowledge beforehand."

"What do you think will happen to him?" Rhonda said. "No wonder Angela and Reggie are so upset."

"That will depend on the case. Perhaps a fine and some jail time. Perhaps having his license taken away. I can't say," said Will. "He's wealthy enough not to worry about survival."

"You and I will have to talk to each other about this on our own. And we're both going to have to speak to Reggie and Angela," said Rhonda. There was a flash of anger in her voice, and I understood it. This might not have happened if everyone had simply talked to one another about it.

Rhonda continued to address Will. "You know how worried I've been about you and your health. You could've had a heart attack and died if you hadn't collapsed. Nothing and nobody are worth losing you."

Will looked like a schoolboy who'd just been scolded by the principal.

I stood. "Look, I'm going to leave you two and go back to the hotel. Rhonda, take as much time with your family as you need."

CHAPTER TWENTY-THREE

As I PULLED AWAY FROM WILL'S OFFICE, I DECIDED TO GO home. We'd talked about the importance of communication, and I wanted to let Vaughn know the situation.

When I got home, Vaughn was down at the sailboat cleaning it up from the last time we'd used it. Some men liked to fuss with their cars; mine liked to fuss with his sailboat.

I called out to him as I walked down the slope to speak to him.

He looked up, grinned, and waited for me to come closer.

When I did, he set down the bucket of water and reached for me.

Our lips met, and I nestled against him, feeling protected and loved and very grateful, most of all, for our life together and how we shared it.

"How are things with Arthur? And how's Will doing?"

"Why don't I fix some sandwiches, and we can talk about it? It's pretty complicated within the family."

"Okay, I'll be up in a minute," said Vaughn. "I want to hear all about it."

Later, after sharing more than lunch with Vaughn, including midday lovemaking, I headed to the hotel and went to find Bernie.

I'd been thinking about Lorraine and our need to support her. She might need privacy. We could provide her with a room at the hotel or, perhaps, she could stay at my house.

With Thanksgiving in a couple of days and the two weddings we had for the weekend, I prayed she'd be able to work and would want to work to keep busy.

Bernie was in his office talking on the phone when I knocked on the door and opened it at his request.

He indicated a chair in front of his desk, and I took a seat to wait for him to finish his call.

"I'm glad you're here," he told me after he ended the call. "As you may have guessed, that was Mike Torson. He and I were discussing a secure place for Lorraine to stay so she wouldn't have to deal with any reporters at her house."

"I've already thought of it. If we don't think she should stay here, she can stay at my house. I've already talked to Vaughn about the possibility. As she's part of our hotel family, we need to protect her."

"Agreed," he said. "She's presently at home. I believe Arthur has posted bail, and he's with her. Would you agree to take them both into your home? I know the situation is difficult with Rhonda and her family, and I don't want to do anything to cause trouble between you."

"Tell you what, I'll talk to Rhonda, and she can decide for me. As you said, I don't want any bad feelings between us and our families."

"That sounds reasonable," said Bernie. "Let me know when you've made a decision."

"Will do," I said and left his office.

Rather than meeting again at Rhonda's house, I decided it was best to ask her to join me here. This would be a business decision, not an emotional one regarding our families. I'd honor her wishes if Rhonda didn't feel it was right.

Before I started the conversation about Lorraine with

Rhonda, I said, "How are things going with Will?"

"After you left, we talked about the situation and the need for us to talk about everything," said Rhonda. "I understand Will didn't want me involved with his business, but he can't let worries almost kill him. In the future, this upset might be a reminder for him."

"And now?"

"He and Reggie will need to smooth out this huge wrinkle in their relationship. It's hard to work with family. Reggie needs to understand that Will made a business decision, not an emotional, hurtful one."

"I can imagine how conflicted Will must have felt when he suspected things were not right with the advice."

"That's it. He didn't want to harm his relationship with Reggie and certainly not with our daughter." Rhonda took out a tissue from her pocket and dabbed at her eyes. "Angela still won't take my calls, and Will doesn't want me to go to their house until things have settled down."

I waited a few moments, and then I said, "Bernie and I have discussed how to protect Lorraine from any harassment. We need her at the hotel to work if she's willing."

"Definitely. For Thanksgiving and the two weddings."

"If Lorraine isn't comfortable staying at the hotel, I'm willing to offer her, and Arthur, too, a place at my house. Vaughn has approved it, but neither of us wants to do anything that might cause friction between you and me. If you feel that having them stay with us would be like taking sides, so to speak, and you don't like the idea, we won't make the offer."

"Aw, Annie, that's so sweet. But as we've always agreed, Lorraine is part of the hotel family. She needs us to help her. This situation must have been a shattering experience for her. No doubt there will be reporters wanting to catch a glimpse of them. Will says Arthur will be allowed to state his case with the SEC and should be given a chance to do so."

"Okay, then, I'll call and make my offer. Heaven knows we need her at the hotel." I rose from my chair, went to Rhonda, and gave her a big hug. "You are a fantastic person. I love you for many reasons, and kindness is one of them."

"Oh, Annie," said Rhonda, grabbing a fresh tissue and wiping her eyes. "We were always meant to be sisters, you know. I just think it took us a few years to find each other."

Now, I felt the sting of tears and accepted the tissue box Rhonda handed me. I'd always wanted a sister, and I couldn't think of anyone better for me.

While Rhonda left the office to talk to Bernie, I called Lorraine. She was hesitant at first to take me up on my offer, but after a brief conversation with Arthur, they both agreed it might be a smart move.

"We'll come in two separate cars and maybe at different times in case the television news truck returns."

"Okay, I'll tell the guard at the gate to our community to look out for you. I'm going home now to get things ready for you. You'll stay in the guest suite, so you can have all the privacy you need."

"Yes, I love your house and its seclusion," said Lorraine. "How can I ever thank you?"

I paused and said honestly, "By helping at the hotel as long as you feel comfortable doing it."

"Deal," said Lorraine. She let out a huge sigh. "I never imagined anything like this. Arthur is devastated."

I ended the call and went to see Bernie.

Rhonda and Bernie were talking when I knocked on the door and went in.

"What's the decision?" asked Rhonda.

"Both Lorraine and Arthur will stay at my house," I said.

"Lorraine has agreed to work at the hotel as long as she's comfortable."

"Thank you, Ann. It was the right thing to do," said Bernie. "If Lorraine feels uncomfortable acting as hostess intermittently with the two of you on Thanksgiving, we'll have Annette do it. Lorraine can help in the back of the house."

"That sounds like a plan. Nell and her family were supposed to come for Thanksgiving. It turned out to be a good thing they had to cancel," I said, thinking of life's twists and turns.

At my house to get ready for our guests, Vaughn greeted me with a kiss. I quickly informed him of the latest news from Rhonda and what was going on with Lorraine and Arthur.

"They want to arrive in their own cars and will get here at different times, hoping no one notices. I've already told the guard at the gatehouse they'll be coming."

"Are Rhonda and Will okay with this?" Vaughn asked.

"Rhonda has agreed to it, and I'm sure she wouldn't have if she thought Will would be upset by it. Angela still won't take her call."

"But it's not Rhonda's fault this happened," said Vaughn, frowning.

"I think it's a matter of divided family loyalty," I said, "but that's something they'll have to work out."

"It's a beautiful day and is supposed to remain that way," said Vaughn. "Do you think Arthur will agree to go sailing with me? I'd rather not stay inside acting as host."

"I bet the fresh air will be enjoyable for him. I don't know how much they'll want to talk about the problem. I've assured them of privacy in the guest wing."

"Okay. Robbie's next door at Brett's house," said Vaughn. He pulled me close and stood with his arms wrapped around me.

I snuggled up against him, feeling the day's tension loosen its grip on my neck and shoulders. I looked up at him, wondering how I could get so lucky. Even my best moments with Robert were never like this.

A call from the gatehouse alerted us to Lorraine's arrival.

I went outside to greet her.

Soon, I saw her car making its way toward me.

I stood at the driveway's entrance, directed her to the guest parking spot, and waited for her to get out of the car.

When she faced me, I understood how disastrous the situation was for her. Usually, a calm, pleasant expression matched the elegant hairstyle and presence she made. Now, without makeup and looking fragile, almost sick, she easily responded to my hug.

"I'm so sorry this is happening, Lorraine," I said.

"Arthur told me it should be over soon, that he had requested the paperwork be done to notify the SEC, and for some reason, his friend's office had not taken care of it properly."

"Come inside. We'll get you settled in your suite. Then we can have a cup of coffee or something refreshing to drink."

Lorraine stood beside me, wringing her hands. "With Thanksgiving tomorrow, I know how much every staff member is needed. I'll be there, too. I promise."

"Let's take it one day at a time. Hopefully, you'll feel like being there. If not, we'll work around it. I don't want to add to your worries."

"Thanks," said Lorraine. "I think the busier I am, the better. I have a lot on my mind right now, and I need time to think things through. Keeping busy will help me." She sighed.

"I need to be there for Arthur too. We've had a healthy marriage, and I know him to be an honest, decent man."

"I totally understand," I said, picking up her suitcase while she grabbed a few bags from the backseat of the car.

We walked inside, and Vaughn met us at the door. "How are you, Lorraine? I heard what happened."

"I'm not doing great, but we'll get through this," said Lorraine.

He took the suitcase from me and led us inside.

I showed Lorraine where everything was in the bedroom and bathroom, and then Vaughn and I left her.

Vaughn gave me a worried look. "Lorraine is really suffering. I like her spirit, though."

"Yes," I said. "It's too bad this has happened. I hope it doesn't harm Arthur and Lorraine's marriage. It's been such a heartwarming one."

A call announced Arthur's arrival at the same time we saw him driving into our driveway.

He parked beside Lorraine's car and got out, standing a moment, gazing around.

A little nervous about meeting him under such conditions, I followed Vaughn outside to greet him. Cindy pranced outside with us, and when she wagged her tail and went right over to Arthur, I felt better. Dogs were sensitive to people and the fact that Cindy liked him meant a lot.

Arthur was as refined in appearance as Lorraine, with classic features. His full head of hair formed a cloud of gray around his head. His eyes, a bright hazel, usually sparkled with interest but now were dimmed, showing his worry. Of average height, he looked smaller and much older than Vaughn, though Vaughn was only a few years younger.

"Hi, Arthur," Vaughn shook his hand.

"How are you?" I asked, giving him a quick hug. "I'm sorry

to hear about your trouble."

"Yeah, me, too. It never should have happened. I think someone reported me, and I think I know who."

"Wait a minute," I said. "You're not implying that the someone was Will, were you?"

Arthur shrugged. "I don't know."

"If you honestly feel that way, I'm sorry, but you can't stay here," I said.

Vaughn's eyes widened. He looked as shocked as Arthur.

"I mean it," I said. "You must know Will would never do such a thing. You have to believe that as part of our family. Do you understand?"

"Yes," said Arthur meekly. "It's something Reggie mentioned. It was about Will not allowing any of their clients to buy that stock."

"Will is a very conservative investor, which is why his clients trust him," said Vaughn quietly. "There isn't a dishonest bone in his body."

"I think his suspicions about the stock were what was eating him alive. He didn't want this to become a family affair. None of us wants that," I said with enough firmness to make it clear.

"You're right," said Arthur, rubbing a hand through his gray hair. "I still don't have all the facts, and I feel like I can't trust anyone right now. This should never have happened. The filings were supposed to be done."

Vaughn clapped him on the back. "Come on inside. Lorraine's already settling into the guest suite."

"Thanks. I don't know how long I'll stay. I'm trying to get in touch with my partners in New York City. One of them is in the same situation."

I followed Vaughn and Arthur inside.

Vaughn led him back to the guest wing while I stayed in

the kitchen. I'd surprised myself by how strongly I felt about protecting Will and Rhonda. But my first loyalty, in this case, was to them, and it always would be.

There was no chance to talk to Vaughn about it because he returned to the kitchen with Lorraine.

"What can I get you?" I asked Lorraine. "Coffee, tea, lemonade, wine?"

"I'd love a cup of black coffee," she said. "Thanks so much."

Arthur entered the kitchen, and Vaughn said, "Hey, Arthur, want to come with me down to my boat?"

"That would be great," said Arthur, looking relieved he wouldn't be stuck talking with the two of us women.

After they left, Lorraine said, "I heard what you said to Arthur. The idea of Will Grayson doing anything like turning Arthur in is absurd. Even though I'm married to Arthur, Will is my personal financial advisor."

"I'm glad to hear how you feel," I said, handing her a fresh cup of coffee. "Let's sit on the lanai. We'll get a view of the men on Vaughn's boat. There's no better place to relax."

We were sitting, not saying much, when I got a phone call from Angela.

I got to my feet. "Excuse me, but I have to take this." I left Lorraine on the lanai and went into the den to talk privately with Angela.

"Hello, Angela. How are you?"

"Not well. My husband is distraught over what happened with his father. It seems Will recently told Reggie he didn't like the idea of advising people to buy it, and now it's become a nightmare for his father. He knows Will would never want to see his father hurt, but they have been so competitive ..." She stopped talking and took a deep, shaky breath.

My eyes widened at the implication. "Will almost died from the stress of holding back his concerns about this stock.

He felt Arthur and others, too, might think of his negativity as a competitive thing between them. I've talked to your mother and Will about this. The reason he kept quiet was that he didn't want it to become a family contest. But he understood he had a responsibility to advise his clients not to buy it."

"Reggie is blaming himself for not talking to his father about it. But how could he? It was confidential business. What am I going to do? I must support both my husband and my father-in-law."

"*And* your stepfather," I said crisply. "*And* your mother. I'm disappointed in how you're treating the best people I know. Perhaps it's time to take a deep breath and think carefully, Angela. You've heard Reggie's concern about what happened to his father, and subsequently, you have refused to take calls from your mother."

"What should I do?" asked Angela. "I trust you to tell me your thoughts."

"I think you should talk to both your parents to have a much clearer perspective from all parties. No matter what, nothing can change the fact that Arthur is caught up in something he shouldn't be. No one wants this to become an issue that could tear the family apart. Lorraine and Arthur are staying with Vaughn and me, with your parents' approval."

"Really? They'd want you to do that?"

"Absolutely. You shouldn't be surprised by their behavior. That's the kind of people they've always been. There are no sides here, Angela. There have been no attempts from either party to do harm to the other. If Reggie feels guilty that he didn't tell his father about his concern about his having inside information, it's something he'll have to work out for himself. I don't think anyone is about to blame Reggie for his father's actions."

"Okay, I'm going to call Mom now. I ... can't believe how I've acted. I wasn't ready to talk to her, but now I am. Thanks, Ann. I love you."

"I love you, too, Angela. You're like my own."

I heard sniffling through the phone, and the call ended.

I sat for a moment in the den by myself. Thinking of all the people I loved, I realized once more how complicated families could be.

CHAPTER TWENTY-FOUR

THANKSGIVING MORNING WAS BRIGHT AND CLEAR, as the weather forecaster had promised. But there was no time to enjoy it. It was the busiest day of the year for the hotel, with all staff helping to serve hundreds of people dinner in several shifts. We did it, in part, because it made such a satisfying difference to many people in the area who'd come to love our expansive buffet.

It made social and foodie news. Turkey wasn't the only meat of the day. A steamship round of beef, halves of ham, and legs of lamb were also offered. Luckily, after several upgrades, our kitchen could handle it.

After our guests had taken what they wanted of meat, vegetables, salads, and desserts and we'd closed the dining room, the staff members could have whatever they wanted of the remaining food. It was a wonderful way to share camaraderie with staff members from all departments.

"Looks like you have a beautiful, sunny day," murmured Vaughn, giving me a last squeeze before I got out of bed.

"It helps when we do. People can spread out to the outdoors to wait until their reservations are ready. What are you doing today until I see you this afternoon?"

"I thought I'd take Arthur for a sail. Robbie and Brett want to come too. It's great that Robbie and Brett can enjoy sailing with me and being on a motorboat with Brett's dad."

I kissed Vaughn and forced myself out of bed. I knew the hotel kitchen staff were already at work.

After I showered and dressed for the day, I went to the

kitchen and found Lorraine waiting for me.

"Ready for a busy day?" I asked, pleased to see her.

"Yes," said Lorraine. "It's essential for me to keep going on with my work even while things are uncertain for Arthur. We talked about it, and he agrees."

"If at any time you feel you can't be part of the scene, please let me know. There's bound to be talk."

"That's why it's important for me to do my usual job. I can't let Arthur's problem ruin my business. He and Vaughn have planned a pleasant day."

I briefly wondered at Lorraine's vehemence and then realized how right she was. She'd worked hard to establish herself as a well-known wedding planner and had spent years alone building her business. It seemed only right that she fight for its continued success now.

We arrived at the hotel to find the kitchen area abuzz with excitement. A small area in Consuela's kitchen, apart from the main kitchen, offered hot coffee and tea, plates of sweet rolls and cookies, and plenty of ice water. We needed the staff to be cared for throughout the day as they'd be on their feet for many hours.

Lorraine and I grabbed cups of coffee and a treat and moved to my office.

Rhonda was already there. "Hi, Ann. Hi, Lorraine. I'm glad you're here. I wanted to be sure there would be no hard feelings between us because of any problems with Arthur."

"Thank you for saying that," said Lorraine. "I've done a lot of thinking about it, and I won't let anything come between my friendships with the two of you."

"I appreciate it," said Rhonda. "After reading more about the situation online on the local TV website, Will thinks

Arthur may be able to work something out. Apparently, he wasn't the only one whose purchase wasn't reported to the SEC by the stockbroker."

"I hope that's the case because Arthur is devastated. He has many big clients whom he'd hate to disappoint."

Lorraine and I sat, and we formed a little circle.

"Naturally, I've been thinking a lot about this, and I've concluded that nothing should come between us," said Lorraine. "We are three smart, successful women who love our spouses, families, and friends. Whatever happens, we can move forward."

"I've thought about that too," said Rhonda. "I know Arthur was disappointed that Reggie chose to go into business with Will. I understand. I get that Will wants to prove to Arthur that his business is successful, but this incident has pointed out how foolish it can be. We should simply want the best for everyone."

"I appreciate your show of support by being here, Lorraine," I said. "I honestly believe everything will work out however it's supposed to."

"Me, too," said Lorraine. She studied Rhonda and me, then blinked back tears.

Seeing her so emotional, Rhonda and I looked at one another with blurred vision. Women were strong. Even stronger when helping one another.

The day was as exhausting as other Thanksgivings and as equally gratifying as requests for rooms and functions grew for the future. But for me, after all the work of providing meals for our guests, it was a time to be together with my hotel family and my own for a quiet late evening.

It was also the day before one of my favorite events of the

year—decorating the hotel for Christmas. In those early mornings following Thanksgiving Day, Manny and his crew erected a large, live tree in the front hallway. Then, the decorator we hired would sweep in with her team, along with some members of our staff, to decorate the tree and fill the nooks and crannies of the public rooms and dining rooms with touches of holiday decorations. The timing was important. We wanted as many of our guests as possible to awake to a completely changed décor.

Each year was a bit different. This season, Rhonda and I chose "The Wonder of the Sea" as a theme. I couldn't wait to see how it would all turn out.

The decorator and her team were due to arrive at eight o'clock.

Though the thought of lingering in bed was enticing, I left Vaughn still asleep and quietly left the house. Lorraine had already gone before me.

When I arrived at the hotel, the decorator's van was already parked behind the hotel. As I pulled into a parking space, the staff from Tropical Fleurs, the florist we used for most occasions, pulled their van next to me. They'd worked with the decorator for years and were part of our annual Christmas project.

"Glad to see you," I said to the gentleman who emerged from the van.

"It's always nice to be here at the hotel. Especially at this time of day when I can grab some coffee and a sweet roll."

I laughed. It was a useful way to bribe service people to come to the hotel early in the day.

I went inside the hotel, leaving him and his co-worker to figure out how to unload the van. In all the confusion of

Bubbles at The Beach House Hotel

Arthur's dilemma, I forgot to check the arrangements for both of the weekend weddings.

I said hello to Consuela, and instead of going to my office, I went to see Lorraine. Vaughn and I had kept to our promise of allowing Lorraine and Arthur to enjoy total privacy, and after an exhausting day at the hotel, I hadn't wanted to discuss business with her.

I knocked on her door and opened it.

Smiling, Lorraine called me inside. "Hi, I'm just going over the details for both of the weddings. Now that the decorator is here, I need to make sure the library is set up for the Saturday wedding. The bride chose a Christmas color theme, which makes it easy. I just need to make sure the details are what she wants."

"And the Sunday wedding? I haven't heard anything."

"It's going to be super easy," said Lorraine. "It's the first time we've had a wedding in one of the houses. The book club group is staying in House #2. House #1 is where the wedding will take place."

"Wow!" I said, surprised but pleased by the idea. "Caro said she and Henry wanted a simple wedding. This is as simple as it can get. What about a theme? Decorations? Flowers?"

"Her color scheme is dark green and white. For the house, we've planned a white basket with a green ribbon and filled with freesia, orchids, white roses, and dark green leaves. After the service, the party will move to the private dining room, where flowers of a similar nature will sit on the four tables. The tables will be covered in dark green linen."

"That will be stunning. I can't wait to see what the bride will be wearing."

"Caro has been one of my favorite people to work with on this," said Lorraine. "The couple truly wants it to be simple

195

and easy. It's a last-minute arrangement, and they don't want to stress about it."

"I wish more couples felt that way," I said.

"Yes, our group tomorrow won't be that easy. The bride is a young, local woman who's spoiled. Some of the guests arrived yesterday for Thanksgiving dinner. Tonight's rehearsal dinner is being held elsewhere, but we'll have the bridal luncheon here tomorrow. We could never have taken a late wedding request for Sunday if the ceremony weren't being held at one of the houses."

"Not with a send-off breakfast at the hotel Sunday noon for Saturday's wedding guests. How about the meal in the private dining room for our small wedding group? Is that going to be easy to do?"

Lorraine gave me a satisfied smile. "Surf and turf for the main course. And some interesting choices for appetizers, sides, and even desserts. Instead of a wedding cake, they want a selection of pastries."

"I can't wait for this wedding. Rhonda and I feel very connected to this group."

"So far, they've been a delight to work with. I've even had requests for champagne to be available on Saturday evening to be served at the house, along with a tray of appetizers and snacks before moving to the hotel."

"This is a group that definitely likes a little bubbly," I said. "When they made their original reservations here, they even talked about bubble baths at the house."

"That's so cute," said Lorraine. "One of the gifts the bride is giving to people in attendance is a package of bubble bath powder from the spa shop."

"Sweet. Thanks for all the input. I've got to see what Tropical Fleurs and our designer are doing with our Christmas decorations."

"See you later," said Lorraine. "I'm glad you're handling that."

"It's always fun and a mad race to get it done quickly," I said, standing.

I left Lorraine's office and went to the front hall, where a beautiful, tall spruce tree was being decorated.

Rhonda was standing in the middle of the hallway with a wide smile. "This is going to be stunning," she said, giving me a gleeful hug. "Look at the ornaments." She held up a sheet of photographs. "There are shells of every size, starfish, beach plum accents, crystals, glass balls, and deep aqua, peacock green, and silver ribbons.

I stared up at the tree, imagining how it would look finished. Right now, sparkly white lights were being threaded through the branches.

"It's always so exciting," I said, watching for a minute. "Do you remember our first Christmas tree here at the hotel? It wasn't as fancy as this, but it was ours, and we were very proud of it."

"I still love seeing the hotel decorated like this. It makes the holidays seem so much more alive."

"I just found out information about the upcoming weddings. Caro and Henry have decided to have their ceremony in one of the houses. It'll be a first for us."

Rhonda grinned. "It seems right for them, somehow. Their relationship evolved so fast not only because of the hotel's atmosphere but because of us."

I laughed. "Okay, if you say so."

"You know I'm right. And it's a relief to laugh after all the crap that has gone on. I hope this holiday season will prepare us for another year without any family problems."

"I agree. Let's have fun."

We followed the directions from the designer's staff and

placed candles, ribbons, and decorations where they told us, feeling a part of the project.

By noon, we were still working when Lorraine approached us. "Arthur called. He's flying to New York City to meet with his lawyers. He's asked me to come with him. I told him I could go on Sunday morning but not before. I figure you two could handle the small wedding for your friends. Is that all right?"

Rhonda and I glanced at one another.

"Of course," Rhonda said.

"Are you alright?" I asked, observing her red eyes.

"I will be," she said. "It's been a rough morning. It will take time for Reggie and his father to work things out. It might be wise for us to leave for a few days."

"I see," said Rhonda, looking worried. "Can I do anything to help?"

Lorraine shook her head. "I think it's something they have to do for themselves."

"Don't worry about Sunday's wedding. But if you and Laura could handle the wedding tomorrow, we'd really appreciate it. You said the bride was spoiled, and the last thing we need is for her to turn into a bridezilla."

"Amen," said Rhonda. "This has been such a terrible week, and I wouldn't be pleasant handling that."

"Understood," said Lorraine. She gazed around. "The tree and decorations are stunning. I'm sure the hotel will be busy for our holiday brunch season because everyone will want to come here to look at them. It's become a kind of tradition."

Lorraine left us, and Rhonda gripped my arm. "Should I call Angela? Do anything for Reggie?"

"I'm afraid this is one time where there's nothing to do but wait," I said.

"You know how I hate that," sighed Rhonda.

"Let's concentrate on the hotel, the staff party, the upcoming events, and the things we can control."

"Okay," said Rhonda. "But I won't rest until I know everything is all right with Angela and her family."

"I understand," I said as my cell rang. *Vaughn.*

"Hi, Sweetie. What's up?" I asked.

"It's Randolph. Stephanie and I are with him at the hospital. He's not feeling well, and the doctor thinks it's time to change the batteries of his pacemaker. Stephanie is pretty upset because she found him on the floor."

"I'll come to the hospital right now." Stephanie and Randolph were the closest thing my family had as grandparents.

"What's wrong now?" said Rhonda.

I told her and sighed. "I guess the more people we include in our hotel family, the more issues we'll have with them."

"But that's being part of a family," Rhonda said, and I was reminded how unusual my own family had been growing up with just a grandmother.

"You're right. No matter what, I'd still want them to be part of it."

"Go," said Rhonda. "I'll see that things are completed here. I'm also going to have Lorraine send each of us the file for Sunday's wedding so we can plan how that will get done."

I grabbed my things and drove to the hospital as quickly as I could.

When I arrived, I saw Vaughn and Stephanie in the emergency waiting room and hurried over to them. "How is Randolph?"

"He's all right," Vaughn assured me. "It's the battery in his pacemaker that's the problem. It needs to be replaced.

They're giving him a lot of antibiotics now and will do the surgical procedure later today."

"A few days ago, Randolph told me he'd called for an appointment to have the work done, but apparently, it couldn't wait that long," said Stephanie.

"I'll stay here with Stephanie until the surgery is complete," Vaughn said. "The procedure isn't difficult. Lots of people can have it done as an outpatient, but they told us they want to keep Randolph overnight."

I gave Stephanie a long hug. "I'll take Vaughn's place after the procedure. We'll have you come for dinner, so you don't have to worry about that."

"What would we ever do without you two?" Stephanie said. "You've given us a whole new life as Robbie's grandparents."

"We feel the same about you. We're family," I said.

"Who knew this would happen when we couldn't get a room at the hotel?" said Stephanie, doing her best not to cry.

"A lucky day for all of us," I said.

"I'll walk you out," said Vaughn to me. "And then Stephanie and I are moving to the surgical waiting area."

"Okay, I'll see you later," I said, waving to Stephanie.

"How are they both?" I asked Vaughn. "Stephanie looks completely frazzled."

"Stephanie had a very frightening scare. Apparently, Randolph just fell to the floor. She thought he was dead. Luckily, Randolph came to quickly, and she called 911. Then she called me."

"It's lucky she knew you were home and that you weren't sailing," I said. "I'll go back to the hotel and wait for a call from either her or you."

"Elena knows I'm here. She'll wait at the house for Robbie to return from Brett's. I asked her not to mention anything to him about Randolph until I could talk to him. I know he'll be upset."

"Maybe he can visit Randolph tonight," I said.

"How are things at the hotel?" Vaughn asked me.

"Busy with the Christmas decorating, but it's going to look lovely. And Rhonda and I are greeting the five women of the book club who are returning this afternoon for the wedding of one of them."

"Don't worry about things here. We don't expect bad news, but I'll be here to support Stephanie."

I hugged him. "Have I told you lately how much I love you?"

"Not since last night," he said, grinning.

CHAPTER TWENTY-FIVE

THE HOUSEKEEPING STAFF WAS CLEANING THE LOBBY from the remnants of Christmas decorating when I got a call from Jane Sweeny that the book club group was close to their arrival.

Rhonda and I went to the front entrance to welcome our special arrivals.

Grinning, Rhonda nudged me. "How many times do you suppose we've done this? Waiting to greet guests has always been exciting for me because we never know what will happen with each visit."

"Life is full of surprises and none more so than here at the hotel," I said to her and looked up as a white stretch limo rolled between the gates of the hotel property.

We waited until the limousine had stopped and then hurried down the front steps to greet our guests.

Jane was the first out of the limousine.

I was startled by the change I saw in her in just a few months. Gone was the streak of gray, replaced by a new soft brown color like the rest of her hair, which was cut into a more flattering style. Her wardrobe had been updated, and with makeup, she looked years younger.

"Hello," she said. "It's fantastic to be back here. And for such an exciting reason."

We hugged, and I turned to Caro, who looked as stunning as ever. Her previously reserved manner was much more open, and her blue eyes sparkled with happiness.

Amy, Lisa, and Heather approached me as a group to

exchange hugs. Talking and laughing all at once, it seemed more like a homecoming of family rather than guests we hadn't known several weeks ago.

When we were finished greeting one another, Rhonda said, "Let's get you signed in, and then we'll take you to the guesthouse. You'll see, not much has changed."

"I hope you have some bubbles waiting for us," said Amy.

"That and some other things," I said. "The bellman will take care of your luggage."

The young man stepped forward. "I've brought the cart right here so we can transfer everything from the limo."

"Please be careful with the hanging bag," said Caro. "It's my wedding dress."

He bobbed his head, and we left him to his work.

As we approached the house, I saw a member of the kitchen staff leave and silently thanked him for his timing.

When we entered the house, seven tulip glasses and a charcuterie board were displayed in the kitchen.

"Yes!" cried Heather. "I've told my friends all about the service at the hotel. This is excellent."

The bellman arrived, and he made quick work of placing suitcases in the right rooms. This time, Caro would have the master suite, and the others would share the two other suites. It gave them all plenty of room.

As soon as the bellman left, Amy said, "Okay, I'm opening a bottle of bubbly. This calls for a very special celebration." She turned to Caro. "We're so happy for you. You and Henry make a terrific couple. We knew it right after you met."

Amy took out a bottle of champagne from the refrigerator and popped it open.

She poured some into each of the glasses and then lifted

her own in a toast. "Here's to Caro."

We all raised our glasses, and then we each took a sip. Though I didn't drink every day, I'd come to love having champagne on certain occasions. This was one of the sweetest celebrations.

Rhonda said, "Caro, tell us how Henry proposed. Were you surprised?"

Caro set down her glass and faced Rhonda. "It was very touching, but I wasn't surprised. We'd pretty much decided from the first time we met that there was something special between us. My ex-husband destroyed my self-confidence, but just talking to Henry made me feel very different. Henry is on the shy side, but he has a lot to say when he speaks."

"And apparently, he's very talented when he doesn't need words," teased Amy, and we all chuckled as Caro's cheeks grew pink.

"It's probably a matter of timing, but we are both so ready for this," said Caro. "We decided there was no reason to wait. We felt that strongly."

"I think it's adorable," said Heather. "After a failed marriage, I knew how right and how different things were with Craig soon after I met him. Happily, he felt the same way about me."

"But this is more than a celebration about me," said Caro. "Jane, don't you have something to say?"

Jane clasped her hands in front of her. "The vacation here and these ladies encouraged me to make some changes." She patted her hair and smoothed down her short skirt. "And I've begun dating a very nice man."

"He's a doll," said Lisa. "A widowed teacher at the school where I'm a guidance counselor."

Jane beamed at us and then turned to Amy. "Your turn."

"Ann and Rhonda, you know how helpful Slade was to me

as I went through a difficult time with the death of my ex. We'd been attracted to one another from the first time we met. Even after he and Henry left to help the vice president with an issue, Slade has been in my life. After many talks and discussions, I've agreed to move in with him in Washington D.C., after the new year. We want to see where our relationship can take us."

"How does your son feel about that?" I couldn't stop myself from asking.

"He's all for it. Life with my husband these past several years has been awful for both my son and me. He knows the marriage wasn't good. I kept thinking I could help my husband until I learned only the person who is addicted can make the necessary changes in his life."

"What will you do in D.C.?" asked Rhonda.

"I'm an accountant, so it won't be hard to find work there. After spending so much time worrying about others, it's freeing to do something for myself. Sure, I'm taking a chance that things will work out. But I want to grab hold of this opportunity for true happiness and see where it takes me, takes us."

"Slade is a decent man," said Caro. "He's been through some tough times himself, which is why I think this is a great opportunity for them both."

"Yes, we've talked about making changes in our group, and we've all decided we should do it in small or big ways, whichever works for us," said Jane. "We have our visit here at the hotel to thank for that."

"It's almost magical," said Heather.

Rhonda glanced at me and then said to the others, "We like to think we have a certain ability to help relationships blossom."

"Like what?" asked Lisa, who was married to her high

school sweetheart. "Like matchmakers?"

There was nothing I could do to stop a self-satisfied smile from crossing Rhonda's face.

"Here's to Ann and Rhonda!" cried Jane, and all five women lifted their glasses.

"Let's go out on the lanai," said Jane. "I want to enjoy the sun."

Heather carried the charcuterie tray, Amy grabbed the bottle of Champagne, and we gathered on the lanai near the pool.

"Ahh, it feels wonderful to be back," said Lisa. "When the men get here tomorrow, they'll discover what they have missed. Geoffrey has agreed to stay for the week. It'll be our first vacation together in a long time."

"I'm glad some of you can stay here beyond the wedding," I said.

"We wanted to have this one day together before family and friends arrive," said Heather. "With all the changes taking place, it seems a sweet way to face them. "And we're glad you're here," said Amy, refilling our glasses.

I'd just started to take a sip when my phone rang. *Vaughn.*

"Hi, sweetie. What's up? Is Randolph okay?"

"He's recovering nicely. I'm going to take Stephanie home to rest, and then she's agreed to come for dinner. I thought maybe you could pick up Robbie and make a short visit to Randolph while Stephanie is away. Also, Lorraine and Arthur decided to return to their own home today."

"Okay. That's probably better for them. Please tell Robbie to be ready. I'll be there shortly."

"Everything all right?" Rhonda asked.

"Yes, a man close to the family just had some minor surgery," I said. "I'm going to pick up my son to visit him."

"We sometimes forget that while we're here on vacation,

it's a different story for you and Rhonda. You have your work at the hotel and your families to fill your time," said Jane.

"You'll come to the wedding, won't you? You and your husbands?" said Caro, looking worried.

"Of course," said Rhonda. "We don't want to miss it."

"Right," I said. "It's one of our sweetest hotel stories."

Geoffrey and Heather's husband, Craig, will be here tomorrow afternoon," said Lisa.

I turned to Jane. "Do you have a date for the wedding?"

Blushing furiously, Jane nodded. "It's the schoolteacher I've been dating. Carl Staunton is his name."

"Some of us will be moving to the house next door tomorrow. The rest of the wedding party has rooms at the hotel."

I rose. "It's a joy to have you all here again. Relax and enjoy tomorrow. And then, Rhonda and I will be handling your wedding."

"It's going to be beautiful. I know it," said Rhonda, smiling at the group. "I hope you have your appointments at the spa."

"Oh, yes. We made sure of it," said Heather.

"See you later," I said to the group and left to pick up Robbie.

At home, I asked Vaughn how Robbie had taken the news that his beloved "grandfather" was in the hospital.

"He was very worried, which is why I think it might be comforting for Robbie to see Randolph."

"And to understand how important it is for family members to support one another," I added.

"That, too," said Vaughn. "I'm going to relax here for a while. I might even take a swim. At the hospital, the waiting is really hard. Stephanie didn't relax until she saw Randolph following the surgery."

"How is he?" I asked.

"Awake and alert and annoyed he has to stay in the hospital. But it's the best thing for him. They need to make sure there are no infections or side effects."

"Okay, I'll take Robbie to the hospital and plan something for dinner. Would you grill fish if I picked up some from the grocery store?"

"Sure," said Vaughn.

I knocked on Robbie's door. At his reply, I opened it. Robbie was stretched across his bed, cuddling and playing with Cindy.

"Ready to go see Grandpa Willis?" I asked him.

"Do I have to go? I can Facetime him instead," said Robbie.

I sat down on the edge of the bed. "It'll make Grandpa Willis very glad to see you. When someone you love is sick, it helps to have those who care about him show their support. We won't stay long, but we will try to see him in person."

"Is Grandpa Willis going to die? Is that why we have to go to the hospital?" Robbie's eyes filled.

I put an arm around him. "Grandpa Willis is fine from the surgery. But one day, he will die as part of living. I don't believe you have to worry about that now."

"I was very sad when Trudy died. Remember, Mom?"

"Yes, I do. We all still miss her. She was a wonderful dog. We remember many happy times with her. That's why it's important to make as many memories and enjoy one another as much as we can."

"I love Grandpa Willis," said Robbie, staring out the window thoughtfully.

"I know. That's why we're going to do this," I said, rising.

"Okay," said Robbie, getting off his bed.

###

As we drove to the hospital, I thought about Robbie as a toddler when we first brought him into the family. He'd been a fussy, difficult child who hadn't known boundaries. But after being with Vaughn and me and learning what was expected of him, he became a delightful little boy. Even now, approaching his teens, he was a very kind person, thoughtful of others.

We went inside the hospital and were directed to Randolph's room in the cardiac section.

When we walked into Randolph's room, and I saw how Randolph's face lit with pleasure at the sight of us, I knew I was right to push Robbie into coming here.

Robbie and Randolph hugged, and then Robbie asked him all about his surgery.

After Randolph had explained the basics of pacemakers and how his had needed new batteries, Robbie was quiet for so long that Randolph and I exchanged glances.

"I think I want to be a heart surgeon when I grow up," said Robbie very matter-of-factly. Randolph and I smiled at one another.

"You'll make a great doctor, Robbie. I'm sure of it," said Randolph. "Thanks so much for coming to see me. I'm going home tomorrow and will be ready for all the holiday celebrations."

"Mom says you're not going to die yet," said Robbie.

Randolph chuckled. "That's a relief to hear."

I hugged Randolph and said, "Stephanie is going to have dinner with us, and I'll bring her back here for a visit."

"Thanks," said Randolph. "It was a lucky day when we had to bunk in with you folks at your house."

"It truly was," I quickly agreed.

###

Later, when Stephanie and I made a brief visit to the hospital, I thought again about the relationship my family had with both Stephanie and Randolph. Though they'd served as Robbie's grandparents for only a few years, I had a closer relationship with them than I'd ever had with my grandmother. Even in dying, she hadn't allowed me to be close. She'd dropped dead of a heart attack while I was out of the house at my college class.

CHAPTER TWENTY-SIX

SATURDAY MORNING, I ALLOWED MYSELF SOME EXTRA time in bed. Lorraine and her assistant, Laura, were handling the wedding. Annette would be there to help. The thought of trying to deal with a fussy bride was very unappealing, especially when I knew how excited I was about Caro's wedding tomorrow evening.

After getting up and dressing for the day, I called Lorraine to make sure everything was running smoothly.

"It's going fine, although all of us on staff can't wait to get this one behind us. The bride feels entitled to order people around, making one demand after another. Laura and Annette will take care of brunch tomorrow while I travel to New York. Why don't you and Rhonda enjoy the day, knowing you'll be busy with the next wedding?"

"Thank you. That sounds wonderful. It's been a hectic week."

After I ended the call, I phoned Rhonda. She was as pleased to follow Lorraine's suggestion as I was. Weddings were a ton of work, and though we were excited to handle the one for Caro and Henry, we knew this break from the hotel would be helpful.

After I ended the call, I refilled my coffee cup and headed out to the lanai. Vaughn was sitting there reading.

"Guess what? I have the day off," I said, sitting on the couch next to him. "Want to play?"

Vaughn laughed at my teasing. "I can think of lots of games to play with you. What did you have in mind?"

"I thought this afternoon, it might be pleasant to stroll through town and look at all the decorations."

"I could do that and then take you to dinner," said Vaughn. "Brett has already been here. He wants Robbie to go to Miami with him. His parents are going to look at a new boat, and he doesn't want to go with them alone."

"And Robbie said yes?"

"He's excited about it. The boys will play some sort of computer game challenge on the way and back. And Charlie is going to let them help with the boat. They're stoked about it."

"Then we have a day to enjoy ourselves," I said, becoming excited about the idea of a date with Vaughn.

Late afternoon, after a swim in the heated pool, Vaughn and I got dressed to go downtown. During these times, Vaughn usually wore a baseball cap and sunglasses to help hide his identity. Our friends in town recognized him anyway but were careful not to draw a crowd to him.

Today, he was wearing a black Tampa Bay Rays hat with his favorite Ray Ban sunglasses, tan slacks, and a lightweight black sweater.

"You're looking mighty handsome," I teased.

He laughed. "I have to try to measure up to my date."

He took my arm and escorted me to his sports car. We'd park close to downtown and get out and walk from there.

Sabal was an upscale small town whose merchants strived to outdo one another at holiday time. Between their decorations and the lights wrapped around the trunks of the palm trees lining the streets, the town looked like a fairyland as we entered Main Street.

We strolled down one entire side, stopping to buy

Christmas gifts when we saw something we liked.

As we started back, Vaughn said, "How about a stop at Al's?"

Al's was a neighborhood bar that had fantastic appetizers. That and a beer for Vaughn and a glass of red wine for me sounded perfect. Besides, it's where the locals hung out. We might run into a few people we knew.

From the outside, Al's looked nondescript—a white stucco exterior with a dark wooden sign announcing "Al's, a Bar."

Many visitors would pass it by in favor of something with a more upscale appearance. And that's how the owner, Al Jolley, liked it. Inside, the wood-paneled walls and simple sea-blue and white décor were attractive and well-maintained.

Vaughn and I walked inside and over to the bar.

Al smiled when he saw us. "Haven't seen you guys in a long time. How are you? Any more movies in the making?"

Vaughn chuckled. "I just finished one. How about you? How's business?"

"Booming," said Al, smiling. "It's that time of year when people are out and about and thirsty."

"I'm glad to hear it," said Vaughn. "Ann, what would you like?"

"I'll go for a glass of Pinot Noir," I said, looking over the drinks menu to see if Al offered something the hotel might be interested in.

"Just an IPA for me," said Vaughn. "We're on our way to dinner in a bit and wanted something refreshing before we finish window shopping."

"Looks like you're doing shopping for real," said Al, turning away to get our drinks.

Vaughn and I were still chuckling when Al returned and set glasses in front of us. After the tense, last few days, it felt refreshing to relax.

I listened as Al talked to others at the bar, but I was content to sit quietly with Vaughn. The ability to have comfortable, quiet times with him was something I always enjoyed.

After a short while, we left for our stroll on the opposite side of the street. Darker now, the lights sparkled even brighter. When we finally made it to Andre's for dinner, we were both carrying packages. The thought of a tasty French meal was my idea of perfect.

Margot greeted us with a kiss on both cheeks and assured Vaughn we had the perfect table tucked in a corner.

We took our seats, set down our packages, and faced one another.

"Thanks for a fun time," I said to Vaughn.

He grinned, lighting his dark eyes. "That's what I love about you, Ann. You make everything enjoyable. Nothing has to be fancy to make it that way. In the world of entertainment, it's difficult to find that."

"We're very lucky to have found one another and to be able to share moments like this," I said. "I still sometimes find myself surprised to realize how much my life has changed."

"Well, hold on. It's going to continue to change. Nell told me she's expecting again. And with Liz pregnant, that's two more grandchildren we'll have."

"I still wish there was some way for Nell and Clint to move here," I said.

"Yeah, I've talked to her about it, too. I think it'll happen someday." He reached across the table and took hold of my hand. "I love my family with you."

"Me, too," I said. Gazing at the presents we'd purchased, I knew the real gifts we had to share were not things but feelings.

###

The next morning, I awoke to a blustery day. The sun was out as promised, but a wind had come up. I thought of Caro's wedding and was grateful she and Henry had chosen to get married inside.

I wanted to get to the hotel to make sure our Saturday wedding guests were leaving and to see what Sunday wedding guests had arrived. Because Caro's was an evening wedding, we had time to smooth out any problems. Lorraine and Laura had put together a spreadsheet that Rhonda and I would follow.

Vaughn was in the kitchen when I walked in. "Hi. Is Robbie still sleeping?"

"He's starting that stage of sleeping in," said Vaughn. "Cindy and I have already had a run through the neighborhood, and now she's back in bed with him."

I grinned. Our boy was growing up.

Vaughn and I took our cups of coffee out to the lanai to discuss the day's activities.

Satisfied that everything was in order, I got up to leave.

Vaughn stood and drew me into his arms. "I'll see you later, at the wedding."

We kissed, and as I left the house, I recalled our wedding day. It was such a euphoric time. Hopefully, this is one wedding that'd go off without any complications.

CHAPTER TWENTY-SEVEN

I DROVE THROUGH THE GATES OF THE HOTEL AND CAME TO a stop. Men dressed in black stood outside talking to Bernie and a security guard. It took me a moment to realize that Amelia Swanson must be coming to the wedding.

I drove on, hoping the vice president's appearance wasn't going to be a problem.

When I went into the kitchen, Rhonda was talking to Consuela.

" 'Morning!" I said, and I gave them each a quick hug.

"It's going to be a busy day," said Rhonda. "Apparently, the wedding party got out of hand last night, and there might be some late checkouts. Thankfully, Caro's wedding party is so small. We'll be able to let her people in their rooms early as requested. But some other guests might not be so happy."

"Do we know how many people have come for Caro's wedding?" I asked her.

"No, but I'm having the front desk prepare a report for us," said Rhonda. "We need to be sure gift baskets have been placed in their rooms. Housekeeping will put them there at the appropriate time."

"We're going to use the second house for the ceremony, right? We need to make sure those guests will be leaving on time."

"Let's walk down there to see what's happening," said Rhonda.

We left the hotel and walked onto the sand. As I stood at the water's edge, I saw that the wind was whipping a frothy topping on the crests of the waves. Though the air wasn't hot, the sky was clear, and the sun warmed my cheeks.

"The weather channel said the wind would calm down as this system passed through our region today, sometime this afternoon."

"I hope they're right. I want this wedding to be perfect for Caro and Henry. Especially now that I know Amelia Swanson is going to be here."

Rhonda shook her head. "I hope she doesn't have another project in mind for us."

I laughed. "I think she simply wants to support Henry and Caro." We'd been so busy talking that I didn't notice Brock Goodwin until it was too late.

"Well, what are you two up to now?"

"Just business as usual," I said.

"Did you hear? I was just elected for another term as president of The Neighborhood Association,"

"I'm sure no one ran against you," I said.

"Yeah, it's great that you think it's important," said Rhonda. "Nobody else does."

"You'll pay for that, Rhonda," said Brock and walked away.

"I'm sorry. I can't stand the man."

"I get it," I said, grateful that Brock had walked off in a huff before Rhonda could get fired up with an F-bomb or two.

We continued our walk up the beach to the path for the guesthouses.

At the house we were going to set up for the ceremony, our guests were swimming in the pool. Worried, I hoped they understood they had to be out of the house by noon.

Next door, Jane and Heather were sitting on the lanai and saw us before we got to the front door.

"Come inside, grab a cup of coffee, and join us," Jane called.

Rhonda and I met them out on the lanai.

"A little windy today. I'm glad the wedding is inside," said Heather. "I heard on the news the wind is going to be around for a while."

"Hopefully, not by the time of the wedding," said Rhonda. "Where's the bride?"

"She's inside, going over her wardrobe for her honeymoon. Caro and Henry are flying to Maui to stay in a house owned by the friend of the vice president," said Jane.

"When do they leave?" I asked.

"Tomorrow afternoon by private jet," Jane said, her eyes sparkling. "It's so exciting."

"It sounds perfect. I'm sure the house will be gorgeous," said Rhonda.

Caro, Lisa, and Amy joined us.

"How is everything here? Is there anything we can do for you?" I asked.

"We've arranged for a limo to take us to get our hair and nails done," said Amy. She glanced toward the water. "If this wind doesn't stop soon, it won't matter what our hair looks like."

"The important thing is we're here together," said Lisa.

"That's right," said Jane.

"We're having flowers delivered to the house next door for the ceremony. We'll have your bouquet delivered there, too," I said. "I assume you're dressing there."

"Yes," said Caro. "Then Henry and I will move to the Bridal Suite." She grinned. "It's all still a dream."

Rhonda and I returned to our office, looked over the arrivals and departures schedule, and went to check on rooms needed for the wedding. With the five women and their guests staying at the two houses, we needed only four rooms. One for each set of parents and one for Henry's brother, and, of course, the bridal suite for Henry and Caro. Amelia would be staying with her sister and Jean-Luc at their house, which had been partially remodeled to accommodate her and her security people.

Three of the four rooms were already empty.

Rhonda grinned at me. "Easy, peasy."

I groaned. "No! Don't say that!"

"You're right. Now, we're doomed to trouble. I should know better."

I opened the notebook and stared at the tasks remaining to be done. Nothing unusual.

Henry's parents were due to arrive. We went to the lobby and waited for them. When we saw our hotel limousine pull up to the front of the hotel, Rhonda and I went down the front steps to greet them.

It was always exciting to meet new people, and I couldn't wait to see what Henry's parents were like.

A smiling, blond-haired woman got out of the back of the limo and stood gazing around. Her husband, standing very erect and with classic features, came quickly to her side.

Rhonda and I moved toward them.

"Welcome to The Beach House Hotel," Rhonda said.

"And for such a happy occasion," I added.

Both of his parents smiled and eagerly shook our hands.

"I'd almost given up on Henry getting married," said his mother. "I'm Cilla Watson, and this is my husband, Chester."

"We're so pleased to be a part of the wedding between Henry and Caro. If you need anything, please let us know," I said.

"We were a bit surprised at the suddenness of the ceremony, but once Henry makes up his mind about something, he moves fast," said Cilla.

"His brother, Mark, is due to arrive a little later," I said.

"Yes. I don't know if he's notified the hotel, but he'll be bringing a young lady to the event. That was a last-minute arrangement," said Cilla.

"No problem," Rhonda said. "Come inside. We'll get you registered."

"We've been able to arrange an early check-in for you," I said as I led them inside while Rhonda took care of seeing that the luggage was handled.

In the office, Rhonda and I went over our list.

While she talked with the dining staff, I called Tropical Fleurs to make sure there was no problem with the flowers for the house and for the private dining room. Then I called the Front Desk to see if the bride and groom from Saturday's wedding had vacated the Bridal Suite.

"They haven't checked out. The bride called and asked if they could extend their stay, and I told them I was sorry, but they couldn't," said the front desk clerk. "Even though I apologized, she became upset and told me they were staying in the room whether I liked it or not. She said her mother would pay for it."

I frowned. "Rhonda and I will visit them. I'll let you know what happens."

I ended the call and went to speak to Rhonda.

A look of determination crossed Rhonda's face. "We've got to get them out of there. If they think they can get away with a few more hours in the room, then they'll try for more. I don't want to take a chance on that happening. Lorraine left a note on her desk that this wedding party was a disaster with them making one unreasonable demand after another."

"I hate to disturb our guests, but I think this is important. Caro and the book club women have planned a little party in the suite before the wedding with both Caro's and Henry's mothers."

"Yes, they wanted everyone to be comfortable with one another before the ceremony," said Rhonda. "Let's go."

We walked down to the end of the corridor and knocked on the door.

"Go away," came a female voice.

"We need to speak to you," I said. "Please open the door."

"What the fuck?" a male voice said.

Rhonda knocked on the door again. "We need you to honor the agreement to leave this room. We have another party assigned to it."

We heard conversation, some swearing, and finally, the door opened. A man stood there with a towel wrapped around him. "Sorry. My wife told me we could stay as long as we wanted."

"I'm sorry, but that isn't true," I said, catching a glimpse of a pouting face in the background.

"Okay, give us some time to pack up," said the man, looking angry.

"Twenty minutes max," Rhonda said.

The man glared at her, but Rhonda and I stood there calmly.

The door slammed in our faces.

Letting out sighs of exasperation, we left to go to the front desk. There were days at the hotel when nothing seemed easy.

Twenty-five minutes later, the front desk called to say the couple in the Bridal Suite had left.

I called Housekeeping to alert them, and Rhonda and I

walked down to the suite to explain how we wanted the rooms set up.

After that meeting, we went to the second house, now being cleaned and decorated for the ceremony. We'd been told that Caro had already moved her things into the house and would change into her wedding dress there.

We arrived to find the three men there with Jane, Heather, and Lisa.

"Hi, we were showing the guys around," said Heather. "I want you to meet my husband, Craig." She indicated a well-padded man of average height with an easy-going, friendly smile. He seemed perfect for his laid-back artist wife.

Rhonda and I shook hands with him and then moved to Jane's beau, Carl. Wearing glasses, Carl exchanged handshakes with us and then turned to Jane, who was beaming. Geoffrey, Lisa's high school sweetheart and husband, had similar dark, curly hair, and I couldn't help thinking about how much they looked alike, like some couples who've lived together for some time.

"Welcome to The Beach House Hotel. We hope you have a pleasant stay," I said to the newly arrived men.

"You've picked a beautiful day to be here. It was windy this morning, but it's calmed down," said Rhonda. "Have fun."

"We will," said Jane. "We're going to walk on the beach."

Later, we checked the house again to make sure everything was spotless. While we were there, a staff member from Tropical Fleurs came into the house. "We've got the van here with the flowers. Is it okay to set up?"

"Yes," I said. "Good timing. We want the flowers to be fresh."

Rhonda and I went over Lorraine's notes about the flowers

and made sure the bouquets were placed exactly where Caro wanted them.

After we were pleased the arrangements were right, we left to inspect the private dining room and drop in at the hen party in the Bridal Suite. It was almost time to get ready for the wedding.

CHAPTER TWENTY-EIGHT

RHONDA AND I STEPPED INTO THE DINING ROOM AND sighed with pleasure. The small room looked stunning, with dark green tablecloths on the tables. Crystal goblets sparkled at each place beside shiny silverware. In the middle of each table was a crystal vase holding sprigs of dark green pine, white orchids, and holly branches to add to the holiday décor.

At the far end of the room, the bar was set up, and next to it was a place for the harpist to sit and play music.

"Seeing this makes me want to get married all over again," gushed Rhonda.

We walked to the Bridal Suite and heard the sounds of laughter before we even opened the door. The "Fab Five" plus Cilla and another woman we hadn't met were all talking.

Seeing the group of women like this, I made a mental note that doing something like this for small wedding groups was a great way to put people who might not know one another at ease.

Caro saw us and came over to us. "This has been such a lovely day already. Come meet my mother."

She led us to a tall, thin woman with gray and white streaked hair who was strikingly attractive. It was very clear where Caro got her lovely looks.

"This is Adrienne Graber. And Mom, these are the two fantastic women I told you about. Ann Sanders and Rhonda Grayson, the owners of the hotel."

"It's such a pleasure to meet you both," said Adrienne. "I applaud women like you who've accomplished so much. I've had my own retail business for years."

"Retail, like the hotel business, has its ups and downs," I said.

"Oh, yes," Adrienne said. "I'd hoped Caro would take over the business, but she's off on her own adventures. I understand how important that is."

"I haven't seen Henry yet to congratulate him," I said. "But he's a lucky man."

"Yes. They both are," said Adrienne. "They make a great couple."

"Thanks, Mom," said Caro. "I'm going back to the house now to change." She turned to Jane. "Ready?"

Jane stopped talking and came over to us.

"I'm Caro's matron of honor," she said, her eyes tearing up.

Touched by Caro's sweet gesture, Rhonda and I led them out the door.

We stayed with them as they made their way to the house. One last time, we wanted to make sure everything was the way Caro wanted it.

When Caro walked in and saw the flowers and the chairs arranged in a circle before the fireplace, she clasped her hands. "Oh my! This is beautiful! I can't believe this is actually happening."

"Has Henry seen this?" I asked.

Caro shook her head. "I don't think so. He, Slade, and Amelia should be arriving any minute, which is why I need to hide in the bedroom to change."

"Okay, we'll leave you to it," I said, and Rhonda and I left.

"I'm going home to change," said Rhonda. "Then Will and I'll return and make sure both musicians have arrived."

"Okay, I'll change and hurry back to make sure Amelia, Slade, and Henry have settled in."

Excited about the wedding, I hurried home and changed out of work clothes into a brown linen dress. The wedding was to be a simple one with the men wearing sports coats and slacks, no ties.

After making sure Robbie was fine at Liz's house, Vaughn and I left for the wedding. He was used to my leaving his side to take care of the supervision of affairs like this. I hoped this would be a positive time for him to chat with Will.

Vaughn and I arrived at the house to find two Secret Service people protecting it. Amelia went nowhere without them. One was an older gentleman, the other a young woman. Rhonda and I had seen and talked to them before.

"Looks like a nice day for a wedding, after all," said Vaughn. They both continued to scan the area.

Inside, Amelia was talking to Caro's mother. Each time I saw her, I was reminded of Amelia's struggles to succeed in the political arena. She could've become jaded or bitter but instead had chosen to remain a lovely, approachable woman who knew how to get things done.

"Hello, Ann. How are you?" Amelia said, coming over to give me a quick hug.

I hugged her back, hoping she didn't have more people she wanted to send to Rhonda and me at the hotel.

As if sensing my feelings, Amelia said, "No more special requests for you. For now."

I chuckled. An excellent politician, she'd always leave the door open to another one. "How do you feel about Henry and Slade both falling in love with women they met here at the hotel?"

"You know how much I love this hotel. It seems appropriate somehow. I'm very glad, though, that they'll continue to work for me."

"Yes, both Caro and Amy will be moving to D.C."

Rhonda joined us. "Hello, Madame Vice-President. It's a pleasure to see you here."

"I'm delighted as always," Amelia said, hugging Rhonda. "It's always marvelous to see two of my favorite women. And today is a special one for Henry and Caro. Henry introduced me to Caro on Facetime right after Caro returned to Pennsylvania."

"Sweet of him," I said, noting more guests were arriving. I left Amelia's side to greet them.

The bride and groom's parents arrived, along with Henry's younger brother, who looked remarkably like Henry, and his date, a pretty, young Asian woman.

At a signal from Rhonda, the guitar player Caro had hired for the ceremony started playing. People hurried to their seats. Amelia took her place in front of the fireplace. Henry and his younger brother joined her, wearing tan slacks, white shirts, and navy blazers.

I noted the way Slade and Amy were smiling at one another and felt that they, too, would find happiness together. Carl, standing next to Amy, suddenly smiled, and I glanced over to where Jane and Caro were making their entrance.

Leading the way, Jane wore a simple, dark green sheath with short sleeves. A white orchid was pinned in her hair and matched the strand of white pearls she wore. Her focus remained on Carl, and I knew how much she loved him.

My gaze turned to Caro, and I felt my breath catch in my throat. Caro was stunning in a crochet lace scoop neck midi-dress that showed off her lovely figure tastefully. Her auburn hair was worn in a loose shoulder-length style. A crown of assorted white flowers lay in a circle on her head.

"Such a beautiful bride," someone whispered.

As she came closer, I could see that the flared crochet-lace skirt had an intricate scalloped hem. And as her back faced us, we could see the buttoned V-back.

I glanced at her mother and saw the tears that leaked down her cheeks.

Henry's eyes filled as they focused on Caro with such love that I felt a sting of tears of my own.

After Jane stepped aside, Henry took hold of Caro's hand and lifted it to his lips before facing Amelia.

Amelia talked briefly about the importance of commitment, and then the vows were exchanged, promising love and support to one another.

We in the group were silent as their words filled the room and our hearts. And when Caro told Henry she'd never felt this way before, we all knew that was true. His love had healed the hurts from the past and given her a new reason to speak like this.

The moment Amelia said, "You may now kiss your bride," Henry swept Caro up in his arms and twirled them around in a joyous circle.

Watching them, we all applauded. It was such a short, simple ceremony, but it was much more moving than one with more pomp and less emotion.

"I've got the bubbles," Amy announced.

She and Slade filled the tulip glasses placed in the kitchen. While they handed them out to the wedding guests, Rhonda and I slipped out of the house and headed to the private dining room to make sure things were organized.

We found the harpist ready to begin playing. A waitress was lighting the candles on the tables. A server was standing behind the bar, prepared for action.

The wedding group entered the room, and soon, it was filled with the talk and laughter from a congenial gathering.

Amelia stood with several of the men, talking about one of her duties. Her bodyguards were in place by the entrance.

I stood with the other wedding guests and participants in the private dining room, filled with satisfaction. Caro and Henry had found one another here at the hotel. Rhonda and I had created a space where guests could be assured of privacy, beautiful surroundings, and excellent service and food. More than that, we and the hotel staff worked hard to provide an atmosphere that encouraged our guests to experience the joy of living each day, even finding love here.

For a lonely little girl growing up, I saw these new friends as family and hoped they'd come back again and again.

Vaughn wrapped an arm around me.

From across the room, Rhonda caught my eye, and sensing my feelings, she lifted her hand in a silent salute to us and to all we'd accomplished.

Bubbles of happiness spread through me. There was no better place to be than at The Beach House Hotel.

# # #

Thank you for reading *Bubbles at The Beach House Hotel*. If you enjoyed this book, please help other readers discover it by leaving a review on Amazon, Bookbub, Goodreads, or your favorite site. It's such a nice thing to do.

For your further enjoyment, the other books in The Beach House Hotel Series are available on all sites. Here are the Universal links:

Breakfast at The Beach House Hotel:
https://books2read.com/u/bpkoq4

Lunch at The Beach House Hotel:
https://books2read.com/u/3GWvp3

Dinner at The Beach House Hotel:
https://books2read.com/u/4N1yDW

Christmas at The Beach House Hotel:
https://books2read.com/u/38gZvd

Margaritas at The Beach House Hotel:
https://books2read.com/u/bMRrP7

Dessert at The Beach House Hotel:
https://books2read.com/u/mV6kX6

Coffee at The Beach House Hotel:
https://books2read.com/u/bOnE7A

High Tea at The Beach House Hotel:
https://books2read.com/u/mgN9AK

Nightcaps at The Beach House Hotel:
https://books2read.com/u/mBA2oy

Sign up for my newsletter and get a free story. I keep my newsletters short and fun with giveaways, recipes, and the latest must-have news about me and my books. Welcome! Here's the link:

https://BookHip.com/RRGJKGN

ABOUT THE AUTHOR

A ***USA Today* Best-Selling Author,** Judith Keim is a hybrid author who both has a publisher and self-publishes. Ms. Keim writes heart-warming novels about women who face unexpected challenges, meet them with strength, and find love and happiness along the way—stories with heart. Her best-selling books are based, in part, on many of the places she's lived or visited and on the interesting people she's met, creating believable characters and realistic settings her many loyal readers love.

She enjoyed her childhood and young adult years in Elmira, New York, and now makes her home in Boise, Idaho, with her husband, Peter, and their lovable miniature Dachshund, Wally, and other members of her family.

While growing up, she was drawn to the idea of writing stories from a young age. Books were always present, being read, ready to go back to the library, or about to be discovered. All in her family shared information from the books in general conversation, giving them a wealth of knowledge and vivid imaginations.

Ms. Keim loves to hear from her readers and appreciates their enthusiasm for her stories.

"I hope you've enjoyed this book. If you have, please help other readers discover it by leaving a review on the site of your choice. And please check out my other books and series:

The Hartwell Women Series
The Beach House Hotel Series
The Fat Fridays Group
The Salty Key Inn Series
The Chandler Hill Inn Series
Seashell Cottage Books
The Desert Sage Inn Series
Soul Sisters at Cedar Mountain Lodge
The Sanderling Cove Inn Series
The Lilac Lake Inn Series
Lilac Lake Books

"ALL THE BOOKS ARE NOW AVAILABLE IN AUDIO on Audible, iTunes, Findaway, Kobo, and Google Play! So fun to have these characters come alive!"

Ms. Keim can be reached at **www.judithkeim.com**

"To like my author page on Facebook and keep up with the news, go to: **http://bit.ly/2pZWDgA**

"To receive notices about new books, follow me on Book Bub:

https://www.bookbub.com/authors/judith-keim

"Sign up for my newsletter and get a free story. I keep my newsletters short and fun with giveaways, recipes, and the latest must-have news about me and my books. Welcome! Here's the link:

https://BookHip.com/RRGJKGN

"I am also on Twitter @judithkeim, LinkedIn, and Goodreads. Come say hello!"

ACKNOWLEDGMENTS

As always, I am eternally grateful to my team of editors, Peter Keim and Lynn Mapp, my book cover designer, Lou Harper, and my narrator for Audible and iTunes, Angela Dawe. They are the people who take what I've written and help turn it into the book I proudly present to you, my readers! I also wish to thank my coffee group of writers who listen and encourage me to keep on going. Thank you, Peggy Staggs, Lynn Mapp, Cate Cobb, Nikki Jean Triska, Joanne Pence, Melanie Olsen, and Megan Bryce. And to you, my fabulous readers, I thank you for your continued support and encouragement. Without you, this book would not exist. You are the wind beneath my wings.

Made in the USA
Middletown, DE
11 July 2025